Seaspring

A novel by

Anya Luz Lobos

Illustrated by Don L. Garrett

1st WORLD
PUBLISHING

Seaspring

彬 彬

ANYA LUZ LOBOS

Published by 1stWorld Publishing
1100 North 4th St. Fairfield, Iowa 52556
tel: 641-209-5000 • fax: 641-209-3001
web: www.1stworldpublishing.com

First Edition

LCCN: 2007925558
SoftCover ISBN: 978-1-4218-9961-9
HardCover ISBN: 978-1-4218-9962-6
eBook ISBN: 978-1-4218-9963-3

Cover Illustration by Don L. Garrett
Cover Design by Anuj Mathur

Seaspring

This book is dedicated to
Miles and Poppy,
to their dear father,
and to all their wonderful grandparents.

Acknowledgements

The author gratefully acknowledges the following people: Veronica Theuma, Mary Ashley, Anne Weinert, Ellen Cook, Judi Wolfe, Beulah Smith and Ruby, Donna Seelbach, Ken Bandel, "Mom and Dad," Donna and Steven, Dennis and Dodie; my primas-hermanas, tios y tias, primos y primas; big Bea and little Bea Meza, Lauretta Lucchetti, Shirley Remmert, Terry Sullivan, Ernie and Martha Asten, Rich Haas, Glen LaCoste, Paul Brown; Mike Creedon, Russ Bragg, Dr. F. Wilder, the gentle Duskins, the Spiers, John West, Susan Tereba, Claudine Cline, Christine Schrum, the unforgettable astronomer Professor Hagar, Dr. David McKinney, Melanie Brown, Evanne Jardine, my Nachita, Grove and the wonderful M. J. Also the following organizations: the Transcendental Meditation Program, the San Francisco and Los Angeles police departments, Friends of the Sea Otter.

And most of all, my parents.

From Honolulu to California, it had been a long enjoyable voyage. The small sailing vessel was only hours away from its destination: the Santa Cruz harbor. Tayako sat on the deck, holding her little five-month-old love, Yoshi, to her breast. Her husband, Terry, sat at the rudder.

To describe the event that followed is almost impossible; so quickly did it happen that there was scarcely time to think, or even to fear. To a gull flying in the sky above the boat, it would have looked and sounded like fireworks. To Yoshi, lying half-asleep, it was as though a burning hot wind had suddenly yanked him out of his mother's arms, throwing him high into the sky. Then came the falling sensation, with eyes closed tight and hands clenched, as though trying to hang onto an invisible rope. And then, the cold splash.

First sinking and instinctively not breathing, then rising and flipping over onto his back—water was familiar to him. Only never had it been so cold and harsh, splashing down on his upturned face and muffling his cries; never had he felt so alone. All he could see was the orange glow of sun pouring through closed eyelids—even squinting was impossible. Perhaps any second now he would feel his mother's hand gently pushing up on the small of his back; hear her soft voice praising him for his skills, encouraging him to arch his back just a little more.

No one came.

No one could come.

A brown sea otter zigzagged through the wreckage as though looking for something of value. Two gulls who had swooped down to peck at a loaf of brown bread floating in the water, were soon joined by a third, and the three of them hurriedly snapped up juicy morsels through the tattered yellow and green wrapper.

From the heavens, seeing her baby still alive and struggling, Tayako uttered a piercing prayer: "Oh please, please oh please, don't let my baby boy drown." So pure was her love, that like a stone dropped into a still pool, her prayer sent ripples in all directions.

The otter, making a sharp turn around one end of the floating mast, nearly crashed into the crying baby. Hastily it swam away from him. "Ugh!" it muttered, "Human pup! Get away!" and headed back through the wreckage toward the distant shore. The three gulls were now screeching, yanking at the plastic bread wrapper in an angry tug-o-war to see who would get the last soggy crumbs. Shreds of yellow and green plastic floated on the choppy waters like wounded jellyfish.

The otter, now almost clear of the wreckage, turned its head to look back. "Perhaps there is something I've missed," it mumbled, "Something to eat, perhaps." It headed once again toward the floating mast. (Oh please…) It swam within feet of the drowning boy. Seeing him splashing about so helplessly, "Yuck! Humans!" it cried. "Serves them right!" (Please oh please…) "Hate them, hate them!" the otter shouted suddenly. (Don't let my…) "Hate them!" it cried again. (Please don't let my baby…) "They killed my…" (Don't let my baby boy…) "My baby…pup!" the otter sobbed, tears streaming from its eyes. "Hate them, hate them," it wailed, this time heading out to sea. Suddenly, it turned around again and darted toward the boy as if to attack. But when the otter reached the babe, its whiskered snout only bumped into the infant's tense shoulder, making his cries, which had gradually weakened, suddenly grow loud and desperate, interrupted only by his own spluttering and coughing. "Let him drown. Hate them, hate them!" the otter shouted frantically, now swimming in circles around the baby. (Please don't let...) "Serves them right!" (Don't let my...) "Hate them, hate them!" it cried.

It has been said that something like this could never happen, not in a million years. It has also been said that with love all things are possible. Love is the reason why this "something" that could not happen, not in a million years, did, in fact, happen; and the frantic otter, still muttering "Let him drown! Serves them right!" wrapped its forelegs around the drowning boy, pulled him up against its tummy and then, floating on its back, pulled him toward the distant shoreline.

*A*female sea otter gives birth to a single pup, about five months after mating. She does this not on land, but on the floating kelp beds. She floats on her back carrying her young pup on her tummy for several months, leaving him to paddle about on the surface of the water only for brief moments while she dives to search for food. Later, the growing youngster will learn to dive for his own food and will swim about independently, though he may choose to stay with his mother until her next pup is born.

Weela took a deep breath, then dove to search for food. The warm summer sun was low enough on the horizon that its light no longer glared off the mirror-like water whose surface sparkled. Amidst those amber sparkles, the human pup paddled about gleefully. He enjoyed being left alone, the whole vast ocean to himself.

Soon came the familiar squeal, "Koko! Koko!" and he paddled toward Weela, who was now floating on her back holding a large flat stone in one foreleg, and in the other, what seemed to him like the most enormous abalone he had ever seen. In reality, it could have been a middling-size abalone, or even a small one, because every time that Weela found food, in her eyes there was an excitement that made it seem like the most enormous of treasures.

She placed the flat stone on her furry chest, then eagerly pounded the abalone shell against it, breaking the shell on the third try. Koko watched the flat stone sink then disappear into the water. Looking up at Weela, he saw her whiskered mouth opening and closing noisily. Presently, she pulled a long stringy piece of food out of her mouth and offered it to him. His three and only front teeth were really not up to the task, nor did abalone taste very good to him. The pieces of clam that she often gave to him, or even the kelp that he nibbled on from time to time, were a lot more appealing. But now it was abalone being held before him and he accepted the rubbery offering politely.

Rolling a stringy morsel in his mouth, he swallowed a tiny piece, then gagged upon discovering that the small piece was connected to a larger one still in his mouth. Soon, the entire mouthful fell into the water where he pulled it back and forth playfully, making swirly patterns. When the feast was over, Weela extended herself into the water and rested there buoyantly, gazing up at the clouds. Koko pulled himself onto her tummy; he nursed, and nursing, fell asleep.

Weela felt happiest when Koko suckled at her breast. At such times her eyes closed, her whiskers twitched, and in her mind she relived all the extraordinary events that had led her to this present moment. Her memories contained much of her strength; and so as she nurtured Koko, her memories nurtured her. She thought of how she had rescued her babe and taken him to the old fallen tree, which floated half in and half out of the bay waters. She thought of how her dear husband Theo had gazed at her first with amazement then pride, that she, of all otters, should choose to rescue and nurture a human child. She remembered how once inside the windless, dry shelter of the fallen tree, the babe had cried frantically, shivered uncontrollably, and angrily pushed

Weela away whenever she pulled him to her breast. She recalled how she had persisted even after all the other otters decided it was hopeless, and in a sad group, headed for their home in the kelp beds, leaving only her and Theo and the human pup.

Her only concern then was that he nurse, because she knew that without that warm nourishment and that restful nurturing contact there could be no survival. The more he screamed, the more she rubbed her face against his and drew her silky body close to his, sometimes lying down and encircling him, as if to form a nest around him. But the baby resisted. He knew what he wanted, and what his heart was longing for did not have fur, or whiskers, or a black nose. The crying seemed endless. She wondered if perhaps it had been a mistake to try to rescue him. There had been a time that she had chosen to abandon an injured otter, a time when a killer whale had done too much harm for the victim to ever thrive again within its damaged body. She wondered if perhaps this also was such a time.

But her doubts would last only a few moments (Please, oh please...) then would fade (My baby boy...) into what seemed like an endless soothing prayer (Please help my human pup nurse....) All the while, the sun had risen to its highest place in the sky, then had slowly descended until its warm orange surface almost touched the cold bay waters. The babe's cries weakened into a repetitive moan. Sleep began to overtake him, and with it came dreams. Dreams of mama drawing him near to her, dreams of the flowing liquid love she always gave him. His eyes were almost completely shut, his lips opening and closing slightly as if suckling on an invisible breast. Weela drew herself close to him. He nursed.

Weela remembered all of this, then raising her head

slightly, she wrapped her strong forelegs around the boy and hoisted him up high onto her chest. How soundly he slept! How steady was his breathing! She did not worry about him now. Letting her head sink back into the water, she hugged him with her furry forelegs. Yes, he had grown a lot since then. Her eyes closed, her whiskers twitched. She knew that someday she would remember this as well.

Sunny days gave way to cooler, rainy days, and those in turn gave way to even chillier days. All the while, the silent morning fog had placed its misty blanket over everything, but now it seemed also to be whispering, "Don't get up yet, it's too cold." Through it all the sun and the moon wove their patterns across the sky. To Koko, it was the moon, with her repeated expanding and contracting, that held the greatest fascination. It seemed to him that with the completion of each cycle she grew a little bigger, revealing to him more of her light and dark designs. And with each growth to fullness, the boy also grew. His three front teeth were soon joined by others on the sides, and when once again the seasons turned and the colder days gave way to warmer ones, Weela found that even more teeth had sprung up further back in his mouth and he could tackle even the toughest meal she would offer.

His life was a sensual life, filled with the oceany taste of abalone, clam and sea kelp. During the warm days there was the cozy feel of the sun as he'd stretch out on top of the old fallen tree to nap, and there was the shivery, invigorating feel of the cool bay waters when he'd dive in to swim or look for food. When the days and the nights were cold, there was the wet wood smell and the secure, windless feel inside of the floating fallen tree; and best of all there was the wondrous, silky feel of Weela and Theo huddled up against him to keep him warm.

His life was a silent life, save for the squealing of the otters, the chattering of the porpoises, the cawing of the gulls.

And best of all there was the wondrous silky feel of Weela and Theo, huddled up against him to keep him warm.

Only occasionally would be heard the clap of thunder, usually muted and far away. Rarely would a fishing boat come close enough for him to hear the put-put of its motor or the faint sounds of men. When this happened, Weela, he and the others would hide.

Koko had many young otter friends that he spent his days playing with; and though they could swim faster than he could, he was usually not far behind as he undulated through the water in otter style. In the beginning he had been the great center of attraction, and his young furry friends had spent days on end carefully eyeing his furless skin, looking into his peculiar ears and gently nibbling on his fingers and toes while Koko shrieked with delight. But as time passed and novelty blended with familiarity, Koko came to be loved by them not for his unusualness, but for his playfulness and his kindness. His straight, almost black hair, now down to his shoulders, and his flat, delicate face with almond-shaped eyes and soft, toothy smiles, became an expected part of their daily adventures.

And so, his days filled with the sensations of nature and the joy of being a part of it, the boy thrived and delighted in all that he learned and did. And when the evening breezes lulled him to sleep, he slept a very special sleep. It was not the heavy slumber of one who is tired and longs to forget, but the quiet repose of one who, even while asleep, is delighting in the sound of the rippling waters, and almost hears within that rippling, nature's quiet whispers.

*I*t was a balmy morning. Koko had stayed asleep longer than usual. His boyish hand, like an extension of the floating fallen tree, bobbed in and out of the water as he slept.

"Koko!"

He sat up. A vision of the kelp beds flooded his mind, then a faint taste of clam…that "almost taste" that comes just before biting in.

"Koko!"

He rolled into the water, sinking deep enough to clear the floating tree's underwater branches, then darted straight toward the kelp beds.

Splashing up between the yellow-green kelp plants he saw Theo. Theo's gaze was intent upon Weela; while she, holding a large clam in her forelegs, smiled at Koko proudly. She had not called his name; she had thought it.

And so, as easily as listening to the rain, or looking at it, or feeling its wetness as it trickles down the skin, Koko found himself sharing the sounds, sights and feelings of the otters' minds. And as easily as turning one's head to look at a passing gull, he found himself regaining his own personal quiet and privacy.

At first he could only hear Weela's thoughts as they gently directed themselves toward him. Then came Theo's thoughts, with their rougher textures and their almost musical wanderings. Soon he was proudly sending out his own ideas, and finally he found himself delighting in the sharing of communications with all his friends.

Words were seldom used, as pictures and soft tugging impulses would say almost all that needed to be said.

It was during the quiet moments spent with Weela and Theo that he gradually came to know a special word—one whose existence seemed to be somehow rooted beyond ordinary experiences. Such a word was Amla.

He had felt the soft tingling glow of it more than once. As an infant, nursing at Weela's breast, he had dreamed through its joy. As an older babe, from time to time, he had been awakened by its presence. Keeping his eyes closed, he had sensed that its radiance extended to everything around him, and that even the gray, faded wood of the floating tree surely was glowing. He had not wanted to open his eyes for fear of ending his experience. It was too wonderful. Weela, Theo, the glow, the hushing sound of it: Amla.

Theo was busy pawing through a pile of moss and pebbles that he had dumped onto one of the wide branches of the floating tree. His wet, finely grizzled fur held tiny and gleaming droplets of water.

"What is Amla?"

"Oh, so you know about Amla."

Koko smiled shyly.

Theo stuffed some of the slimy mixture of plants and pebbles into a hole in the tree.

"There, maybe that will keep the rain out," he said spiritedly. "Uncle Enir used to refer to Amla as the Natural Historic Records, but your mother has taught me that there is much more to it than that. Perhaps she is the one you should be asking."

"What is historic records?"

Theo smiled at his son's eagerness. He paused awhile, looking at the sparkling afternoon water.

"Each moment leads to the next moment, my Ko. We do not see the past moments, but they are there, like the flat stones we toss back into the water after pounding our food on them, they are there for us."

"The happy moments?"

"Yes."

"What about the sad ones?"

"Yes, they are there also." Theo looked thoughtful. "But why bother with the sharp spines of the urchin when you can have the tasty meat inside?"

It was fitting that Theo should make such a comparison; his teeth were a pinkish purple as a result of having eaten copious quantities of urchins.

Once again, Koko felt its presence. Amla, he thought, then wondered if Weela and Theo were there beside him. He knew that it was night time and that he was inside the hollow, fallen tree. He remembered having cuddled with his parents as he was drifting off to sleep, his hand lightly tracing along the tree's curving wall. In a dreamy stupor he had rolled away from them seeking the comfort of his favorite nook. An image from a dream he'd been having still lingered in the boy's awareness. In this dream, he'd been swimming through the kelp beds, chasing an enormous spotted fish. Then the fish had become suddenly infused with light, nearly disappearing into its own brilliance. It was this intense brightness that had awakened Koko, even though his eyes had remained closed and his body hadn't budged.

Lying quietly in his nook, Koko listened to the water as it lapped at his floating, branchy home. He noticed the warm and familiar sensation of smooth wood pressing against his cheek. Although awake, he could still barely see the dream fish's translucent tail emitting a warm radiance. He sensed that this radiance was Amla, for he could feel a serene aliveness all around him.

Yet the boy would not open his eyes, even though he was curious to see what effect Amla's presence might be having on his surroundings. He had felt this same hesitation many times before, a concern that even the slightest movement of his eyelids might make his cherished radiance disappear. The thought crossed his mind that, maybe, if he opened his eyes only slightly, the glow would persist, unaffected by a movement so small. He opened his eyes, just barely, peeking at his surroundings through long, thick lashes. He could see it now, with his eyes! The same glow that he had witnessed in his dream. He saw Theo, then Weela. They were sitting not far from him, leaning restfully against one of the tree's walls. Then his eyes caught sight of someone else! There was a tiny brown otter nursing at Weela's breast. Who could this little pup be?

When Koko awoke, the orange glow of the rising sun was already pouring through all of the cracks and holes in the floating hollow tree. It was no surprise to him that Weela was already gone; she was an early riser. Theo was lazily weaving through the water, occasionally brushing past strings of giant kelp that had been floating next to the tree since the evening before. Their long brown fronds and tree-like masses swept over and mingled with some of the floating tree's branches. In one foreleg Theo held a large piece of crab.

"There's plenty for both of us," he said, but Koko's thoughts were not on food.

"Do you know which way Weela went?"

Theo pointed with his eyes. "Off in the shade of that cloud," he replied, "where the ocean looks patchy...do you see her?"

Koko rolled into the water and rubbed his face gently on his father's furry neck. Then, all but disappearing under the water's surface, he undulated toward where Weela was.

He found her floating on her back, her eyes half-closed, her broad flipper-like feet swaying gently in the saffron-colored sea. He could not bring himself to ask his most pressing question, so he asked something else instead.

"Is Amla kind of like remembering?"

She gazed at him with the hesitant look of one who does not want to say no. She licked his chin lovingly, then looking into his eyes, she smiled as he treaded water beside her.

"What can be remembered," she said, "can also be forgotten. Once forgotten, it is gone from our minds. But Amla is there, whether we remember it or not."

Perhaps now he could ask.

"Who is the baby, the one who…"

"You saw Herme, did you?"

"But isn't Herme the one who…"

"Died. Yes, my firstborn."

He had never before approached her on this subject.

She paused, waiting for the right words to come.

"We do not see him in present moments," she said, "only in Amla."

"Then, where is he now?"

"I do not know." She looked at him thoughtfully. "Some of our elders have known such things; perhaps I'll know when I am older."

"Well, what if right now a giant killer whale is trying to eat him!"

Weela had to laugh. It was the husky mature laugh of a forty-five pound otter.

"Did you know, my pup, that sometimes when you are fast asleep, Theo and I huddle very close to you and admire you?"

"You do?" Koko's tan face showed the hint of a blush.

"Whether he is even aware of us," said Weela, "whatever his circumstances, he is nurtured by our love."

The sun had risen at least twice its own width, and its warm orange hue had grown paler, yet also brighter, making

Koko's and Weela's eyelids tighten into a slight squint.

"The people, the ones in the boat; why did they…."

Like the shadow of a passing seagull, a pained look came over Weela's face and then was gone.

"We do not know," she replied. "They had been so friendly on previous visits." Then, sensing Koko's concern about his own humanness, she added, "We were not looking closely, my pup. Maybe it was the same boat, but not the same people."

"But why would any people want to hurt the otters?"

"Perhaps some day you will find that out," she sighed, then gently curved her slick body to form a tight arc around him.

The boy was growing. His tawny body was almost as long as Weela's. "My young kelp plant," Theo would playfully call him, referring to the seaweed's fast-growing nature. It was not unusual to find that a kelp plant had grown two full otter's arm lengths from one morning to the next. Koko and his friends would often play around these giant plants, weaving through and hiding behind their tree-like branches. Some of the plants were so long that twenty otters forming a chain could not equal their length.

"Will my Ko grow as long as the kelp plants?" Theo would ask kiddingly, and even though the boy would laugh, in his heart there was a growing uneasiness; soon he might be longer than all of the otters.

"Why should it matter?" he would ask himself. "I've always looked different."

And having so many friends to play with, and so many things to do and learn, it was easy to put his concern aside, while giving himself over to the happy oblivion of his daily games and explorations.

But sooner or later, the same feelings of uneasiness would come over him. The smallest things would make this happen, like glancing at his own hands as he emptied out a clamshell or seeing his own broken reflection in the bay waters.

Koko's disquiet took on the quality of an unsinkable piece of driftwood when the warm days returned once again and brought with them the beach crowds, with their furless bodies and their fingered paws, their chattery sounds and their brightly colored clothes. Koko and his friends would spy on them from behind the jagged rocks that rose out of the bay near one of the beaches. Over the water's glare he and his companions would stare at them, watching them splash in and out of the water or recline on the sloping sands.

⌣

There were days, usually several in a row, when Koko would stay behind with Theo and Weela, rather than join his friends as they went out to look at the beach crowds. If his parents were not feeling particularly playful, he would play by himself, weaving here and there between the kelp plants or collecting dozens of tiny kelp bulbs and then watching them bob up and down in the water in expanding clusters.

Other days, usually also several in a row, days when perhaps he felt more self-confident, he would join his friends in their daily outings. Once having gotten to their rocky hideout, he would usually end up staying there, long after they had all tired and left. There he would crouch, gazing at the humans, completely engrossed in their games, their sounds, their varied appearances. He would return home only after the sun had all but disappeared into the water and only a handful of people remained walking on the darkened shore.

"Did you have a good day?" Weela would ask as he slowly dragged himself up onto the floating tree.

"Yes," he would answer distantly. For now, his view of human life had to be his own private treasure, to be enjoyed only by himself. And what a vast treasure it was! There were the puffy flat things that floated like jellyfish on the water and carried their passengers lazily this way and that. There were the brightly colored suns that would get flung high into the air and which, when they landed on the sand, would bounce up again like porpoises. There were the big circles that some of the children would wear, making them look as bright as the orange king crabs.

On some days, usually two in a row, the humans would come in enormous crowds, like schools of anchovies. But most of the time their gatherings would be much sparser, allowing Koko to pay more attention to the smaller details: the glossy liquids these humans put on their skins and the noise-makers with stems growing out of them that some of them carried.

Most of the faces would change from day to day so that his memory of one day's gathering would fade into his enjoyment of the next day's. There were a few faces, however, that he would see repeatedly, often in small groups or families and usually in the same spot.

There was one family in particular that always drew his attention. The mother was usually sitting on the sand in the shade of a giant, tan circular structure that the father would expand each morning when they arrived at the beach, and then contract each evening before they left. She was usually involved in gazing at flat connected surfaces that she would open and close like clam shells. Her hair was brown and wavy and hung down to her shoulders, and she always wore the same bright yellow covering over her slender body.

By her side, and usually encircled by a criss-cross wooden structure, was a chubby, tan-haired baby girl who played almost continuously with various colorful objects that her mother had handed to her. The father was a slender yet somewhat muscular man with wavy hair that ended just below his ears and an abundant brown mustache that curved down his face gracefully, much like an otter's whiskers.

But it was the fourth member of the family that captivated Koko's attention: a young boy, perhaps the same age as he. His hair was wavy and light brown, his skin was a golden tan, and he busied himself continuously on the sand right at the water's edge. His father would often join him there, and together they would dig enormous holes and build giant sand structures using colorful containers that they had brought down to the water's edge with them. From where he watched, hidden behind the rocks, Koko could hear their shouts and their laughter.

One day when Koko arrived at his usual hiding place, he was disappointed to find that his "family" was nowhere in sight. He waited for hours, hoping for a late arrival, but the waiting proved fruitless. The appearance of some muscular men carrying an orange puffy boat distracted him for a while. The boat's motor would not start. The men stood knee-deep in the water, the boat gently scraping their legs as it swayed to and fro. They spoke in loud voices as they pointed to the sea, then to the shore, then back to the sea again. Finally they picked up the boat and, carrying it on their shoulders, disappeared over the sand dunes. By this time, the sun had almost set. In the encroaching darkness, Koko felt sad and alone.

"Will my Ko grow as long as the kelp plants?"
Theo would ask.

Tracing the shoreline with his eyes, he saw only a few people. To one side, far away, his eyes registered the silhouette of a man throwing a stick. A large furry creature splashed into the water after the stick. Grabbing it with its mouth, the creature returned it to the man. The boy had seen several such creatures on the beach before, playing that same game, and he had often wondered what kind of relationship they shared with the humans. Turning his head in the opposite direction, he saw two people arm-in-arm, weaving slowly away from him. Looking directly at the closest part of the shore, there was no one, save for two sand crabs skittering sideways on the sand.

It was something he had often dreamed of. Now, almost like an outsider, amazed at his own daring, he felt himself swim toward the shore and, upon arriving, dig his fingers and toes into the cool wet sand beneath him. He ran on its smooth wet edges, and jumped on its powdery surfaces. Then, falling exhausted, he cupped his hands and dug a hole, just like the humans did.

They looked like little shells with sharp, wavy edges. Most of these tiny, circular containers had a soft moon glow, though some had a golden hue. Their outside surfaces displayed a variety of colorful designs, and a few of them were soft and spongy on the inside. The best part of all was that if Koko placed them carefully in the water, they floated.

"I've never seen shells like that," commented Theo, bringing a smile to the boy's face. Nothing pleased Koko more than dazzling his parents with his collection of treasures. He kept most of them hidden away in one of the hollow branch holes of the floating tree: the spongy brown and white shoe, long enough to accommodate two of Koko's feet; the bright, crinkly globe that would not puff up no matter how much he blew into it; the red swimming trunks, just like the ones the boy children wore. Inside the hollow of the floating tree, Koko would put them on sometimes, when no one was watching. On one side there was a pocket that made a loud raspy sound when he pulled it open.

Koko was perched on top of the floating tree, dipping his cupped hand into a puddle of rainwater that had formed on one of the tree's sunken surfaces. It was a lazy evening and the moon's light glistened like wet silk on the bay waters. Even the gulls looked drowsy as they rocked back and forth on the water like feathered driftwood.

"I made a friend today."

"Did you?" Theo asked softly.

"He has hair like mine, only it's a golden brown, like Bren's."

Bren was a baby otter that had just recently joined the otter group.

"It must look very pretty," Weela commented.

"He's very nice," Koko went on, bringing his cupped hand to his lips. The rainwater was cool and sweet. "He makes a lot of sounds with his mouth."

"Then maybe you will learn his language," Weela responded.

The boy with the light brown hair was busily adding more wet sand to a small mountain of sand that he had been working on for most of the morning. A light blue translucent plastic cup had been shoved, face up, into one side of the mountain, and coming out of the cup was a cream-colored string that gracefully trailed down the side of the mountain and then disappeared into a rusty red and silver flashlight. The flashlight had been dismantled and reassembled in such a manner that the string was now a permanent part of it.

Koko came up to the boy and kneeled down before him.

"This is my great big mountain," said the boy.

Koko smiled.

"And see this tunnel over here?" Pointing to the cup, "This is where my sixteen skunks live. Well, they're really nineteen skunks now, 'cause they had quadruplets. Can you imagine that? See them way in there?"

Koko touched the smooth rim of the cup with his finger.

"Well, it's really not a tunnel. It's really a cup, but the skunks think it's a tunnel so I gave it to them 'cause well, you know, skunks love to play in tunnels!"

Koko smiled again.

"Yup, they sure do all right. And this is my 'mote control," he said, pointing to the rusty flashlight. "And see way, way in there next to the skunks, that little shiny thing, way in there? Real, real little? See it?"

Koko leaned forward to see as the boy pointed to a tiny, silvery piece of gum wrapper inside the cup.

"Well, that's the skunks' TV. So now all I have to do is make a great big lake 'cause, well, you know, TVs are electric and you know how important water is for electrics!"

Koko smiled once again.

"Only I have to be very careful, 'cause electrics are very dangerous. I mean very. So well, hey, would you like to help me make a lake so the skunks can watch Scooby Doo? Well, isn't that a great idea? You dig on that side and I'll dig on this side. There you go."

"This is my great big mountain," said the boy.

"It's lunch time Miles!" Barbara called. "Do you think your friend would like to join us?"

The boys had spent the last three days playing together. Barbara knew that Miles' friend didn't speak English.

"Oh sure he would," said Miles, motioning to the boy to follow him to the shade of the big parasol.

Reaching into the green picnic basket, Barbara pulled out a sandwich and handed it to Koko. She then pulled out one more for Miles, and a bowl filled with potato salad for Poppy. A stubby white plastic spoon jutted out from the mound of potatoes. Poppy grabbed the bowl eagerly and placed it on her lap. Wrapping her chubby little hand around the spoon, she poked several holes in the potato mound then started eating heartily. Only two sandwiches remained at the bottom of the basket.

"This one doesn't have pickles," Barbara explained as she handed Tim one of the remaining sandwiches. Then she took the last one for herself.

Koko watched Miles carefully, then held his own sandwich up to his mouth and bit into it. A bright yellow liquid oozed onto his chin. He took another bite. It was delicious.

Later that day Barbara said to Miles, "It's so nice that you've found a friend." She made this comment as she and the rest of the family walked back to the beach house where they were staying. And off in the darkening bay as Koko climbed up onto the floating tree, Weela and Theo echoed the same feeling.

Koko would now spend all of his early mornings playing with his otter friends, and then he would swim to the shore to spend his late mornings and afternoons on the beach playing with Miles. The otters seemed to understand Koko's need and never complained about his long daily departures.

And so the days and nights passed quickly, and the moon's gradual growing, then shrinking, was hardly noticed by either of the two boys, who slept so very soundly.

One day, Tim was trying to learn the boy's name. "Barbara," he said, pointing to his wife, then "Miles, Poppy," he pronounced, pointing to his son and then his daughter. Touching his own chest with his index finger, he said "Tim." Then, pointing directly to the boy, he asked, "Now, what's your name?"

The boy had never heard humans make otter-like sounds so he modified the otter pronunciation. "Ko Ko," he said softly.

"Koko," repeated Tim. "Did you hear that, Barb?"

"Koko," said Miles.

"Sure did," answered Barbara.

"'Ko' is a real popular name ending in Japan," added Tim.

As the weeks passed, Koko's one-word communications grew to include more words, which in time joined with one another to form statements and questions.

"Koko is really learning English," Tim commented one

day, as he listened to the two boys' distant chattering.

"I just hope he doesn't forget his own language," Barbara responded.

One late August morning as the summer drew to a close, Miles eagerly awaited Koko's arrival.

"I wonder where Koko's parents live," Barbara mused, as she changed Poppy's diaper.

"Oh, probably in one of the beach motels nearby," answered Tim.

"Nope," said Miles matter-of-factly, then pointed straight out to sea. "They live out there," he said, "only we can't see them from here."

Tim and Barbara looked at each other questioningly.

"Oh...of course!" said Tim, gently hugging Miles' shoulders, "Koko's homeland *is* way out there. After all, his parents are surely Japanese."

"Oh what a smart boy you are Miles!" praised Barbara, giving her son a hug. The boy was bursting with pride.

"Do Japanese eat seafood?" he asked.

"Why yes, they do," answered Tim.

That afternoon as Miles and Koko played in the sand, digging long canals at the water's edge, Miles said, "I found out what your furry parents are called."

"What?" asked Koko.

"Japanese."

"*I* have to leave," he said shakily.

"I know," she answered. A single tear came down her furry snout.

"Tomorrow they go inland. I don't know when I can return. Tell Theo I...."

One by one she licked the tears from his face, then, softly treading water beside him, she rested her head next to his.

"Amla," she thought.

"Amla," he answered.

*I*t had been almost two weeks since the family had returned from its long summer retreat. Barbara had been very busy getting the house back in order while Tim had been working long days at a new building site. Apart from the fact that Miles had been eating much more than usual, everything seemed back to normal. It was a Sunday morning. Miles was busy playing in the toy room with a new dinosaur puzzle that Tim had brought home the night before, and Poppy was sitting in the big wicker rocking chair in the living room, rocking back and forth contentedly. As Barbara washed the last of the breakfast dishes, Tim sat at the kitchen table enjoying his fourth piece of buttered toast.

"Tim, do you think you could rake the leaves in the driveway?" Her tone was melodious.

"Sure," Tim answered.

"I think the rake is way out in the backyard, near the maple tree."

"OK," said Tim, and letting the kitchen screen door slam slightly, he headed toward the far end of the backyard, humming as he walked.

The yard was longer than the house was. It bordered a wide canyon so that there were no neighbors behind the house, only to the sides. It was the beautiful view of the canyon that had convinced them to buy the house in the first place, and now Tim was looking forward to enjoying the view.

"The maple tree," Tim uttered under his breath while looking at the giant willow that loomed up in front of him. "Oh, behind the willow," he smiled. He glided through the willow's leafy and curtain-like extensions, then stumbled and almost fell. Regaining his balance, he looked down to see the cause of his near fall.

"Koko," he said, smiling vaguely, "what are you doing here?"

The boy was wearing Miles' striped yellow and white sweater and his checkered tan and green shorts. A brown blanket rested on the weed-covered ground next to him. Tim gazed at him, trying to take the whole picture in, then picked him up and, holding him in his arms, quickly carried him toward the house.

"Barbara! Miles! Come here!" he shouted.

Barbara came running out of the house with Poppy on one hip, while Miles followed several feet behind them.

"Koko!" she exclaimed, looking at the boy in astonishment while Miles looked sheepishly at the ground.

"Miles, how did Koko get here?" Tim asked sternly.

"Well..." he said, "there was plenty of room under the back seat of the van."

"Oh, my Lord," said Barbara, "his parents must be worried sick."

"Miles, why did you do this?"

"Well, I've been giving him lots of fresh air and sunshine."

"Miles."

"Well...I just didn't want to not see him anymore," the boy said brokenly, tears streaming down his face.

"I can't believe this has happened," said Tim. "We'd better call the police."

Now, Koko also burst into tears, and Tim, still holding him in his arms, sat down at the shady picnic table that rested just outside the back door.

"There, there, we'll find your parents, everything will be fine," he said, hugging the boy as he spoke.

"But they said it was OK," Miles uttered through his tears.

"Who did?" asked Barbara.

"His parents!" he answered with a whine.

"They must have thought he was just coming for the day," Barbara explained, "not for two weeks!"

"Besides, Miles," Tim said sternly, "you're supposed to ask us for permission, not other people's parents. And you aren't supposed to hide things from us."

"But I asked if he could live with us and you said no," Miles cried.

Barbara sat Poppy down on the picnic bench, then positioned herself next to her. She pulled Miles onto her lap.

"When Mama and Dada say 'no,' Miles, they have a good reason. We love Koko very much, but his parents also love him, with all their hearts, and he belongs with them."

"But they really did say I could live with you." Koko spoke for the first time, tears still running down his cheeks.

"Koko..." asked Tim, "aren't you happy living with your parents?"

The boy caught his breath. "I'm happy," he answered.

"Well, isn't there enough food for all of you?"

"Lots of food," he answered.

Now it was Barbara's turn to ask:

"Are they too sick to take care of you?"

"No."

"Then tell us why they'd want you to live with us?"

The boy caught his breath again.

"They knew I had to live with people, like me."

"You mean with other children?"

"No, just people."

"Yeah," said Miles, "he couldn't just spend his whole life hiding with the Japanese."

"What?" asked Tim.

"Wait," Barbara interjected suddenly. "I think we're getting somewhere. Koko, are your parents hiding?"

"Only from the people," he answered.

It seemed like an odd answer, but then the boy had only been speaking in English for about two months.

"Do you think you can take us to the house where your parents are hiding?"

"They don't live in a house."

"Well, where do they live?"

"In the ocean," Miles said a little impatiently. "I told you that already."

"Miles, you let Koko answer. Where do your parents live, Koko?" Barbara asked again.

"In the ocean."

Visions of Japanese boat people hiding off the coast of Monterey flooded her mind.

"If we went with you back to the beach," she said diplomatically, "do you think you could show us where their boat is, so that we could all visit them?"

"They don't live in a boat."

"Well, what do they live in?" asked Tim, completely intrigued.

"Well," answered Koko, "they sleep in a floating tree."

There was a long silence.

"Ah," Tim finally said, "Is the tree real long and sinks down deep into the water, then comes up again?"

"No, it just floats," Koko replied.

"Well," said Barbara, following Tim's submarine, "the boy can't be more than four years old; maybe he didn't realize that it was under the water sometimes." Then to herself she wondered why such a little boy would be traveling in a submarine.

"They only sleep in the tree when I'm there," the boy went on, trying to clarify his previous statement, "so I don't get too cold."

"Well, where do they sleep when you aren't there?" Tim asked curiously.

"In the seaweeds," answered Koko.

"You mean, where weeds and plants grow near the sea?"

"Isn't it seaweeds that float in the water?" he asked, feeling a little confused.

"Yes, that's right," answered Barbara.

"Well, that's where they sleep."

"On little boats or rafts?" Tim asked hopefully.

"No, just on their backs."

"Wow!" sighed Miles enthusiastically. "What happens if they roll over when they're asleep?"

"They don't usually roll over."

"What is going on here!" exclaimed Tim, suppressing an urge to pound his head on the picnic table. He and Barbara looked at each other blankly. "We'd better call the police," he said, and with a frightened Koko still in his arms, he stood up and headed toward the kitchen door.

"Wait," said Barbara, "let me try something first."

They all followed her as she marched into the kitchen and walked over to the wall phone. Holding the receiver up to her head, she pushed three numbers.

"What is the area code for the Monterey area?" she asked. There was a pause after which she hung up and dialed again. This time she pushed eleven numbers.

"May I have the number of the Monterey police department?" she asked. After another brief pause and a short "Thank you," she hung up and once again pushed eleven numbers.

"Hello," she said softly, "My name is Eileen Harris. I'm not sure, but maybe you can help me. Our home is in Iowa. Well, my husband just got a job opportunity in the

Monterey area, and we've seen so much on TV about child abductions and things like that—and we're just wondering how safe a place the Monterey/Santa Cruz area is for us to raise our children." There was a long silence.

"Well, thank you officer, you've been very helpful. Goodbye." She hung up the phone, then looked at Tim.

"In that entire area, there hasn't been a missing child that hasn't been somehow accounted for in over ten years," she stated.

"So, Sherlock, what do you conclude?" Tim's voice had a slight edge.

"Well, now we know that Koko's parents haven't reported him missing, at least not to the Monterey police," she answered. "Maybe his parents really are hiding," she added thoughtfully, "or maybe, for some reason, they really did want him to come with us."

"That's what I said," exclaimed Miles.

There was a huge bowl of grapes on the kitchen table and Miles was looking at it.

"Can I share this with Koko and Poppy?" he asked.

"Of course," answered Tim, patting his son on the back for the first time since that morning's discovery.

Tim looked at Barbara. "There could be other explanations, Barb," he argued the point. "Maybe there's been a big mix-up. Maybe his parents thought he was going to spend a few weeks with some other relatives who were also at the beach. Maybe his parents haven't even realized he's missing yet. Or maybe Koko got lost someplace other than Monterey —long before this summer, even—and then just ended up in Monterey somehow. Barb, maybe the boy is all confused because of all he's gone through."

"I guess you're right," Barbara replied a little dejectedly, "I suppose there could be lots of explanations."

"Koko," asked Tim, "did your parents really know it was us you were coming to live with? Is there someone else they might have thought you were going with? Some other friends or family?"

"I never met anyone else on the beach," he answered slowly and thoughtfully, "They knew it was you."

"So tell us again Koko," Barbara asked, "why did your parents say it was OK for you to come live with us?"

"'Cause I couldn't be my whole life playing with the Japanese. I was getting too big. I needed to be with people like me."

"Now that makes a lot of sense!" exclaimed Tim, a look of exasperation on his face.

Tim and Barbara sat there in silence. The two boys and Poppy eagerly plucked the green grapes from their vine, leaving little grayish bare branches underneath.

"Miles," Tim finally said, "you seem to understand this better than we do. Can you explain it to us?"

Miles looked thoughtful. This was his big chance to set things straight. He put a handful of grapes down on his lap, where Poppy wouldn't see them.

"It's simple," he began, "Koko and I want to be brothers, and they thought it was OK, 'cause he needs to be with people and not just Japanese!"

Tim looked at Barbara dumbfoundedly. The kids had just about eaten up all of the grapes.

"One thing is for sure," Tim commented. "If this whole thing is a lie, it's one they both believe."

Barbara jumped out of her seat. "Don't do anything," she shouted, then ran downstairs to the study. A few minutes later she came back, holding a magazine in one hand. The magazine was folded open and on its exposed page was a picture of a young Japanese couple standing in front of a colorful pagoda. It was an advertisement for a Japanese airline.

"Maybe this picture of a Japanese couple will bring back some memories," she reasoned.

"Let me see," said Miles eagerly.

"Koko, does this picture remind you of anyone?" asked Barbara.

The boy smiled delightedly. He had never seen humans that looked so much like himself before.

"But where's their fur?" asked Miles.

"Maybe these are my first parents." Koko stared at the picture unwaveringly, seeming mesmerized.

"Your first parents?" Tim and Barbara asked simultaneously.

"They died...in a boat explosion," he said quietly. "I was a tiny baby. Weela told me about it."

"Who is Weela?"

"She's my Japanese mother. She saved me."

The longest of silences followed. Even Poppy looked thoughtful as she stared out into space, too full to eat any more grapes.

From where he sat, looking through the kitchen window, Tim could see the lime green willow swaying in the wind.

He barely heard Miles repeat his question.

"But why don't they have any fur? Are there different kinds of Japanese?"

And he barely heard Barbara's answer.

"Well, Miles, some Japanese people have darker skin and bigger bodies. Some of them might have longer hair and beards or mustaches."

None of the pieces seemed to fit. The new revelation that Koko had lost his parents when he was a baby didn't really help matters any. And why did the boy keep saying that he needed to live with people like himself? Tim thought of one more question.

"Does Weela look *kind of* like these people?" he asked, pointing to the couple in the magazine.

"Uh uh," the boy answered.

"What does she look like?"

"Well," said Koko, picturing her in his mind, "she has very shiny eyes, white whiskers, soft dark fur, and a black nose. She's very beautiful," he sighed.

"Does Weela look like this?" asked Barbara, pointing to a picture in a book.

"No, that's a dog!" Koko answered with a laugh, as though someone had just tickled him.

Tim's head tilted as he looked at her. She knew what he was thinking: "Barbara, let's not insult the boy's intelligence!"

"Sorry," she said, shrugging her shoulders slightly, "just testing."

Poppy was busy pulling books down from all of the shelves in the study. She had never been allowed to do that before. Now suddenly the rules had been changed and everyone seemed delighted with her occupation.

"That's my good baby!" cooed Barbara reassuringly from where she sat next to the large table in the study.

"How about this picture?" Tim asked, pointing to a small drawing on one of the pages of the family encyclopedia.

"No," answered Koko, "they don't have horns."

"Tusks," corrected Miles, "when they point down they're called tusks."

"Oh!" said Koko.

No one bothered to comment on Miles' definition.

"Well, at least now we know that his parents aren't walruses," commented Tim.

"How about this picture?" asked Barbara, holding open a large book that she had just pulled down from one of the top shelves of the family library. The book was called *The Life of the Sea.*

"Do your parents look like this?"

"Kind of..." Koko answered, then added, "but do these have legs and arms?"

"Do seals have legs and arms?"

"Barb...."

"Well, I thought maybe they were hidden in their fur."

"Let me take a look," said Tim, pulling the open book over the table's slick, wooden surface. Turning the pages hastily, he came upon a picture of a California sea otter floating in the water.

"That's like them!" Koko pointed excitedly, "That's like my Japanese!"

Tim and Barbara looked as though they had just solved the world's greatest mystery. Finally they were getting somewhere. The whole idea was entirely preposterous, but at least now it made sense.

The rest of the afternoon was spent double-checking. Tim and Barbara found one more book about the sea, and as Koko kneeled on the oak chair that faced the large round table in the study, they sat at each side of him quickly turning pages and asking him questions.

"Do your parents break the big shells with their teeth?"

"No, they hit them on a rock."

"That's right!" exclaimed Tim, sounding like a quiz show host.

"Did you ever see this kind of seaweed?" Barbara asked, pointing to a picture in one of the books.

"Uh, I've never seen that kind."

"That's right!" she exclaimed. "Laminaria only grows in Arctic waters."

Miles had grown tired of all the questions and answers and was now building giant towers out of books. Poppy, sitting on top of a large mountain of books, looked at him drowsily.

"How about this kind of plant?"

"Uh huh."

"That's right!" the voices continued.

Poppy's eyes closed, her head dropped slightly and then raised up again as she regained her balance.

Poppy had fallen asleep while nursing. Barbara gently placed her on the king-size bed. On the other side of the large French doors that connected Barbara's and Tim's bedroom with the kids' room, Tim was standing by the bunk bed with the boys. Miles wanted the top bunk, so Koko took the bottom one. Since he had never slept in a bed before, Koko didn't feel the least bit cheated at not getting to climb the ladder.

"You boys have a good sleep," said Tim, giving each of

them a hug. "And no trying to stay awake, you hear Miles?"

"OK, Dada." He spoke in the subdued tone that always preceded sound sleep.

When Tim returned to the bedroom, Barbara was sitting comfortably, her back propped up against a giant, pale green velour pillow that she had placed at the head of the bed. On the far side of the bed, Poppy lay fast asleep. A little thermal blanket covered her chubby legs.

Tim looked at his watch. "Great time for an afternoon nap," he sighed.

"They'll just sleep through until morning," Barbara said softly. "Did you give them some fruit and yogurt before putting them down?"

"Uh huh," he answered, "I had some too." Then turning to look at her, "Aren't you hungry?"

"I had an apple and some cheese about an hour ago."

Barbara turned the knob on the bedside light to a dim setting, then, sinking into the green velour pillow, she stretched out her arms and looked at the shadows. Only Poppy's fuzzy snores disturbed the silence. She leaned over and gave Tim a kiss.

"It's been such an incredible day," he whispered.

"I know. It kind of reminds me of when I went to visit my relatives in Virginia—you remember, the ones I hadn't seen in over twenty years?"

"I remember."

"I couldn't believe I was really seeing them after all that time; even while it was happening, it seemed like a dream —even now, as I think about it."

"You were floating on clouds for about three days after that visit." Tim paused. "I wish we were floating on clouds now."

Barbara put her head against his shoulder. Tim spoke again.

"The boy seems so sincere, Barbara. But do you think his story can really be true?"

"It all seemed so believable just an hour ago," she sighed, "but now, as I think about it.... Tim, do you think maybe he experienced some sort of a trauma at some time, and as a result of that, his mind has fabricated this whole thing?"

"If that's so," Tim answered, "then the boy's a genius."

"I know. He's got every detail down perfect, down to the last seaweed."

"The boy did learn English awfully fast, though," continued Tim, "Maybe he really is a genius, and maybe his parents are marine biologists or something like that. That would explain his vast knowledge about sea otters and sea vegetation."

Since their discovery that the boy had not been reported missing in the Monterey/Santa Cruz area, Tim and Barbara had been avoiding the subject of calling the police. Already they were feeling guilty about having waited this long.

"The whole thing is confusing, Barb. Maybe I'm being naïve, but the boy's sincerity haunts me. What if what he has told us really is true?"

The idea that certain animals might be able to communicate telepathically was not a completely foreign one to Tim; from time to time he had come upon such concepts while leafing through some of the more avant garde scientific journals and periodicals. Usually such ideas were not taken too seriously by mainstream scientific thought; but they made for some very interesting reading that Tim had occasionally involved himself in. It made some sense to him that if animals didn't have the physical ability to speak, then perhaps some of them might have the more subtle ability of speaking with their minds. But whether or not this was actually the case had never been a pressing question to him, at least, not until today.

Now, suddenly, he was sharing his home with a little boy whose sincerity was unquestionable, whose knowledge about sea otters was uncanny, and who claimed that these very same creatures—with individual names, no less—had rescued him and raised him as one of their own. Had the boy said that he had been raised by whales or dolphins, Tim would have been disinclined to believe it. But after reading about the way of life of Enhydra lutris (the sea otter), he was not so sure, particularly since this animal's way of raising its young displayed all of the devotion and constant care, which is so necessary to the raising of a human child.

There were other parallels that had also impressed him: the birth of usually only one pup (or cub), and the mother's continued show of affection to that pup even after it had been weaned. Combining these findings with the average weight and size of these gentle creatures, it no longer seemed impossible that a human child could thrive under their nurturing care. This was especially so if, as Koko had revealed, the parent otters had taken up residence in the hollow of a tree in order to protect the child from the chill of the water and air. And even such a move, to a dry and windless residence, did not seem unlikely, as sea otters had originally spent more time on land and had gradually been driven farther into the sea by their growing fear of humans.

In one of Miles' nature books, Tim had seen a picture of

a goldfinch mother rearing a baby cuckoo two times its own size. Apparently this is a common occurrence as European cuckoos habitually lay their eggs in other birds' nests, with no intention of ever returning to them. On a television documentary, Tim and Barbara had seen Russian swimming instructors dropping six-month old infants into icy waters as part of the training program. There was no doubt about it: the world was full of strange happenings. And as unlikely as Koko's story appeared to be on the surface, Tim could not dismiss the possibility that it might be true.

Such a possibility appealed to him; he wished that somehow Koko's story could be investigated and proven. But he was also aware of all the pitfalls that, to his own way of seeing things, were an inevitable part of such detailed inquiry.

"If his story is taken seriously, can you imagine all of the chaos that will follow? All the investigations and publicity?" His eyes connected with Barbara's momentarily. "If there's one thing I've learned over the years, Barb, it's that people will do just about anything to capitalize on a good story—no matter who it hurts."

They sat there in silence. Tim looked to the far side of the bed where Poppy lay sleeping. She had squeezed a corner of her little blanket into a clump, which she was holding pressed against her lips. "Barb...if his real parents can't be found, do you suppose they might let us adopt him?"

Barbara hugged his arm tightly. She had been hoping he would say that. "Maybe they would," she answered.

They had gone to an adoption agency once years ago, long before she had become pregnant with Miles. The experience had been a trying one for both of them. After answering hundred of questions about their income, their philosophy on child-raising, their lifestyles and their religions, they had left the interview feeling like poor risks, with incomes that didn't flow, attitudes that weren't sufficiently ordinary and religions that didn't match.

"We have more money than we did then," he said. But thinking about adoption was like planning an outing without knowing the condition of the weather, and trying to understand Koko's true origins was not nearly as easy as letting up the shades and looking out the window. "Barbara," he said thoughtfully, "maybe you were on the right track when you called the Monterey police department. I mean, maybe it's just a matter of expanding our search." He paused a second. "Aren't there records that we could get a hold of somewhere, you know, with pictures of missing children from all over California?"

Barbara's forehead wrinkled slightly. "It seems like it should be possible," she mused. Tim could almost see the ideas taking shape in her mind. Barbara loved playing detective. She felt a wonderful sense of exhilaration and freedom whenever she did, perhaps because on such occasions she could bend the law without feeling that she was doing something wrong.

"I bet they have hundreds of pictures at the San Francisco police department," she said. "I'd just have to give them some good reason for wanting to go through them." She looked to Tim for encouragement. "Do you want me to look into it?"

"Do you think it's a good idea?" asked Tim, feeling a little guilty about having originated such a plan.

"Well, don't you?" she asked, throwing it back on his shoulders.

"Oh, I don't know, Barb!" She could feel the weight of responsibility in his voice. "I just don't want the boy to get hurt, that's all." She waited for his answer. "I don't suppose it can do any harm for us to do some research on our own for awhile."

Tim was exhausted; so was Barbara.

"I'm so tired I don't even know what makes sense any more," she said. "But I do know that I'd like to do that tomorrow."

"Well, good," he sighed. "At least we have some sort of a plan." He looked at his watch. "I've got to get some rest," he said.

Barbara leaned over to kiss him. Then, sinking once again into the soft velour pillow, she closed her eyes.

When Tim closed his eyes he could hear his own thoughts tossing about like broken branches in a hurricane. Only at the eye of the storm, at his own center, was there any quiet.

"Tim, wake up."

"Huh?"

"Tim," she whispered again.

It was Barbara.

"I talked to the San Francisco police department."

Tim sat up quickly; he was almost awake.

"I'm driving the van in. You'll watch the kids?"

He looked at his watch. It was six-fifteen in the morning. Everyone else was still asleep.

"Barb, what did you tell them?"

"That I'd seen a little boy at a shopping center and that his face had reminded me of a picture on a missing child poster that I had seen somewhere in California while we were traveling this summer."

Tim was too drowsy for such a long sentence.

"Anyway, it turns out that the missing persons bulletins are available to the public. I just have to go to the Missing Juvenile department and tell them the age group I want to look at. Only I have to go right now 'cause I might have to fly to LA."

Now Tim was ninety-nine percent awake.

"LA?"

"Just in case Koko got lost in the LA area."

"Wouldn't the records in San Francisco cover that?"

"It turns out every major city has its own collection of bulletins," she replied. "There's some overlap, but we couldn't be sure without checking."

"But Barbara, LA..."

"It's OK, Tim," she interjected reassuringly, "it's a short flight. It'll take me longer to drive to San Francisco than it will to fly from there to LA."

Had Tim been more wide-awake, he wouldn't have been as surprised by his wife's flurry of activity. She was that type of person. Once she got onto a project, there was no stopping her.

"Barb, you'll need money."

"It's all right," she assured, then kissed him on the lips. "I took the $300 from behind the book shelf."

It was getting late. Tim put his magazine down on the

ground next to him. The house's shadow had slowly crept over the back yard so that now even Poppy was surrounded by its coolness as she played in the sandbox. On the far end of the yard, toward the canyon, Miles and Koko were taking turns riding around the trees on Miles' little bicycle. Tim looked up toward the house. From where he sat, on the old tree stump that rested on the ground near one corner of the sandbox, he could see the sun's light glowing, halo-like, behind the house's wooden shingles. He stood up and started walking toward the boys. Then, hearing the back door open, he turned around. It was Barbara.

"I found a child that looked a lot like Koko," she said in a tired voice. "Then I discovered it was a girl."

Poppy ran across the sand and over the sandbox's wooden rim to the grassy spot where her mother was standing. Barbara looked at her as though she were a long lost friend, then sat down on the grass next to her. The baby climbed into her arms and immediately started asking to nurse. Barbara undid the top button on her pale cotton blouse.

"No one else came even close," she added. "Or if they did come close, their present ages were nowhere near Koko's age."

Off in the distance, the boys were laughing as they took turns riding through the willow's curtain-like branches.

"Are you sure, Barbara?" Tim asked, sitting down on the grass next to her.

"Oh, I'm quite sure," she replied. "I was very thorough. I even read the written descriptions of children whose faces weren't shown. But new pictures and descriptions come in all the time," she added. "Oh, Tim, it was so sad seeing all those pictures of missing children." Tim's eyes met hers briefly; he understood how she had felt, and she knew that he did.

"Fortunately the police department's filing system is computerized, and Koko's Oriental appearance narrowed things down a lot. Otherwise I don't know how long it would have taken. As it was, the officers who helped me spent a lot of time getting additional information from the local centers for missing children."

"Were you asked a lot of questions?"

"Not really. I just pretended to be looking for that imaginary boy in the shopping center. Everything went smoothly." She paused. "Tim, I just feel so guilty." She pressed her quivering lips softly against Poppy's warm forehead. The baby was almost asleep.

Tim put his arm around his wife. "Barb, if you think we should tell the police, then maybe that's what we should do."

"That's the whole problem," she sobbed, "it doesn't seem right to tell them. Nothing seems right." She brought her hand up to her face and wiped the tears from her eyes. Her voice was so broken that Tim could barely understand it. "All we're doing is trying to find his real parents, and keep him from getting hurt just in case they can't be found." She took a deep breath. "Of course I want him to be a part of our family. I mean, in a way, it would break my heart if we found them, but we wouldn't let that stop us."

"Of course we wouldn't," he agreed with her. "We couldn't live with ourselves if we did."

Tim kneeled in front of her. Then, leaning forward, he kissed her on the cheek. "Tell me, Barb," he said, "if we told the police right now, how would you feel?"

"I'd just feel so terrible, Tim; like we had somehow betrayed him."

"Worse than you feel now?"

Barbara thought for a few seconds.

"Uh huh," she answered, "I think so."

"More guilty?"

"I think so."

"Well, then, you're doing the best you can, Barb," he said in a fatherly tone. "No one can ask more of you than that." Tim turned his head to look toward the canyon. He could barely see the boys as they stood talking in the shadows. "Barb, I'm not ready to make any big decisions, but until I am, until we both are, how can it be wrong for us to learn everything we can? After all, this isn't a clear-cut situation."

Barbara put her hand gently around his neck, then slowly withdrew it. She was still crying a little, but now there was a wet smile on her face as well. "You're right," she said. "It's just that I'm one of those people who'll stand..." Her voice was unsteady and difficult to follow. "...stand at an intersection and wait for the light to turn green..." Tears were pouring down the sides of her face. "...even if the nearest car is two miles away!"

"Oh Barb, I love you."

"Pizza, Pizza!" shouted Miles as he ran toward the front door with Poppy shrieking right behind him. Their early evening nap had obviously restored their vitality and stimulated their appetites. Even Koko was excited, though he had never eaten pizza before.

"Did you get one with bell peppers and one with no bell peppers, Dada?"

"Sure did," answered Tim, carrying two pink boxes in

his arms.

The children sat eagerly at the kitchen table while Barbara placed slices on each of their plates. Tim poured the milk into their cups. Then after filling his own cup, he picked it up and took two steps toward the living room.

"Mama and Dada need to talk some," he said to them. "You have a quiet, happy dinner, OK?"

Miles nodded.

"Ok," answered Koko. He was the only one whose mouth wasn't full of food.

Barbara, holding a plate in each hand, followed Tim into the living room. She was looking amazingly composed, compared to the disquieted state she had been in earlier. In fact, ever since having come out of the bedroom, where she and Poppy had napped together, Barbara had been positively beaming. Tim found his wife's quick recoveries somewhat disconcerting, in spite of the fact that it was usually his words of encouragement that helped bring them about. He also rested during the kid's nap time, but now the burden of all the day's unresolved questions was hanging heavy on his mind. From where he and Barbara sat on the sofa, the two of them could see the little trio dining happily. Miles was pulling his slice of pizza away from his mouth to see how far the cheese would stretch before breaking. Soon Koko and Poppy were following his example.

Tim looked thoughtful; his face was serious.

"Let's assume that no one can find his real parents," he started.

"All right...." Barbara nodded.

"It doesn't guarantee that we'll be the ones to adopt him."

"That's what I'm afraid of,"she replied.

"If his story is believed, he'll probably end up being adopted by some childless cultural anthropologists who applied to adopt a child years ago."

Barbara envisioned two elderly anthropologists holding the boy's hands and walking off with him into the sunset. The vision was humorous. But she knew what Tim was trying to say and she listened quietly.

"And if his story isn't believed, he'll probably be surrounded by child psychologists for years to come."

"I guess that really could happen," she commented thoughtfully.

"You know, Barbara, I can hardly believe I'm saying this, but I've been talking to the boy today, and I'm beginning to think that his story might really be true."

Tim's words made Barbara feel all quivery. The magic feeling of the previous day's question and answer session came back to her. For those three hours, as she and Tim had leaned against the round oak table and listened to Koko's answers and descriptions, she had been completely convinced of the truth behind his words. It was only after her doubting mind had had its say that her basic belief of the boy's story was shaken. Now, she thought about how extraordinary it would be to grow up in the sea, surrounded by its silence and its freshness, nurtured by some of its most gentle creatures. And as her mind drifted with that vision, she saw Koko's life as quite naturally reaching out from that nurturing beginning —toward the land and toward human parents who would understand his unique connection with nature, and not try to sever it. Maybe the whole thing was just that simple, just that perfect.

Tim's voice drifted into her awareness. He was in the middle of saying something, but she wasn't sure what it was. Maybe his meaning would become apparent with his next words.

"And if that's the case," he continued, "then the otters actually chose us to care for him." Tim was surprised at hearing his own words. He was talking about the otters as though he had personally spoken to them. He knew that he had gone too far.

When it came to ponderous matters, it was Tim's nature to make bold statements, then retreat from them as though they had been made by someone else. And it was Barbara's nature to, at first that is, keep her convictions safely tucked away inside herself, where they would secretly grow and intensify. Then, when Tim made a statement that she fervently agreed with, she would cling to it with the tenacity of a barnacle, so that between his retreating and her hanging on, they created an atmosphere of a tug-o-war. Tim knew this pattern all too well, and his most recent verbal overstep had reminded him of it. While he had been speaking, he had noticed that Barbara looked somewhat distracted. Now he was hoping that perhaps she had missed his last sentence completely, as this would get him out of the tight corner that he had stepped into. But when he looked into his wife's eyes, instead of seeing distraction he saw a look that revealed deep emotion.

"Oh Tim," she said hugging him, "that's exactly how I feel. This boy has been placed in our care. We can't betray that trust. If we aren't able to find his real parents, then we're going to have to figure out a way of raising him ourselves."

"Wait a minute!" Tim exclaimed. "Let's not go so fast."

And the tug-o-war began.

Presently Barbara's trembling voice could be heard by the children. "But you said..." she sobbed, sounding like a child herself.

It is a well known fact—among parents anyway—that children can be like little magnifying glasses, so that if the parents are having a minor disagreement, the children will also become argumentative. But if the parents are having a deeply emotional encounter, the children may become like little cannibals who have just lost their cooking pot.

After several pizza wars, the boys plunged into a "spinning" ritual, which consisted of each of them holding a pizza box and then spinning around as fast as possible until all the left-over pizza crusts came flying out. All the while, Poppy cried and cried, still remembering the slice of pizza that Miles had taken from her. It was she who saved the evening by running into the living room and throwing herself desperately into her mother's arms.

"We've done it again, haven't we?" sighed Tim.

"We sure have," Barbara replied tearfully, then swaying Poppy from side to side, she spoke to her in soothing tones until her loud cries faded into soft whimpers. When Tim offered Poppy his last slice of pizza, her recovery was complete. In the kitchen, the boys echoed Poppy's contentment by sitting quietly together on the floor and making a pizza crust face.

How quickly children change. So great was the contrast between the previous moments of agitation and the present ones of silence that it seemed as though a hushing layer of snow had fallen over everything and everyone. The next time that Tim spoke, he was surprised at how loud his own voice sounded. As Barbara responded thoughtfully to his ideas, the conversation took on a fresher quality—no longer like tugging but rather like carefully pulling, from different angles, on a knotted piece of string in order to untie it. As the whys and hows of Koko's predicament became more clearly understood, Tim and Barbara found themselves considering a plan.

It was Barbara who first thought of this new strategy, and what it lacked in substance it made up for in complicated twists and turns, so that Alfred Hitchcock himself would have surely given up before solving its mystery. But even Barbara regarded the scheme with skepticism, and it wasn't until she and Tim elaborated on it, inventing a Japanese father and an infirm Mexican mother, an overburdened aunt with a homeless orphan, and unusual circumstances with untraceable origins, that it all started seeming quite credible.

One very good thing about the plan was that, in spite of being intricate, its application was basically simple and did not require complicated explanations to the children. It relied heavily on the fact that most adults don't take what children say too seriously and that children can be asked (though not completely trusted) to refrain from speaking about certain things in public. There was but one unremembered aunt, with undetermined whereabouts, whose existence the children would be led to innocently accept. And since neither Tim nor Barbara had ever told the children that there really was a Santa Claus or a tooth fairy, they hoped that perhaps they were entitled to this transgression.

Who knows how parents make decisions, anyway? Like south-bound birds: with their eyes they may be studying the landscape, while all along they are really following the promptings of their hearts. Tim and Barbara's strategy included such things as a proximity between Koko and his otter family, a continued search for his original family and, if this search proved fruitless, eventual legal adoption. All of these goals pulled on the caring parents with the irresistible charm of a warm breeze. It was only a matter of time before they noticed that they had been swept away in a decision —not a completely comfortable decision, but the only one that either of them could make.

When Koko woke up, it was daybreak. He looked up at the top bunk and saw one of Miles' feet sticking out slightly over the edge of it. He climbed out of bed and tiptoed toward the window. Looking out, he saw the long backyard with its pine trees, oak trees and wildflowers. Far off in the distance was the lime green willow, barely moving in the wind. The sky was an orangey pink and there were wispy, translucent clouds thinly covering it. Then, turning his head to look through the large open doorway, he saw Tim, Barbara and Poppy, still asleep on the large bed.

Barbara shifted her weight just a little, letting one arm settle softly on Poppy's mint green thermal blanket. Then raising her arm once again and scratching her chin with her fingers, she opened her eyes slightly and saw Koko. Smiling at him she gestured with one hand for him to come into the room. When he got to the foot of the bed, she patted her right hand, the hand nearest to Tim, on the chenille-covered mattress, so he would climb in between them. The bed was soft and yielded like cotton under the weight of his hands and knees.

Tim looked at the boy through the corner of his eyes and, raising his arm, he cupped the boy's shoulder with his hand and shook it gently. Then, using the same hand, he patted the bed, just as Barbara had done, so the boy would lie down.

Barbara pulled her side of the soft chenille bedspread up and over his legs and arms, then moving her hand toward his forehead, she stroked it once gently.

Turning his head from side to side, Koko could see their smiling faces. Soon their eyes were closed again, and then his eyes closed also. A warm feeling filled his heart.

They were like radiant suns glowing at each side of him.

All of the things that Miles and Poppy had been fascinated by as young crawlers, Koko was delighting in now: the lathering with shampoo, the climbing of stairs, the rocking in rocking chairs, the flipping of switches to make lights go on and off. Barbara felt as though there were a new baby in the house and this made her happy.

But it was in the evenings, after having had dinner, that Koko felt most settled and at home. Tim and Barbara would sit in the living room and talk quietly, while Poppy, who was usually at her best when her tummy was full, would amble through the house, picking up toys as she went and playing with them happily.

Sometimes Barbara would take her guitar out of its dusty case, and sing songs to her family. One song that would inevitably be requested by one of the younger members of her audience was a song that Miles had written:

> Thistle, thistle, thistle,
> I don't want my popsicle.
> Thistle, thistle, thistle,
> I don't want my rocking chair, 'cause it's broke.

What followed beyond that first verse was different each time Barbara sang the song, for inevitably she would have to interrupt her guitar playing in order to incorporate Miles' new inspirations.

There was another song, one that Tim and Koko would usually request. It had a slow flowing rhythm that reminded Koko of his life with the otters. His favorite parts were the long choruses:

> If you close your eyes and listen,
>   you can see the waters glisten,
>   watch the sea kelp,
>   tossed like salad
>   by the tumbling sea.
> Waves that curve like celery stalks
> crunch along the rounding rocks.
> Swaying waters, will I leave you?
> Dancing waters, will you let me,
>   ocean waters?

Tim's favorite place to sit was the tan padded sofa, while Miles, sitting cross-legged on the floor just below him, would lean into his father's legs.

> If you close your eyes and listen,
>   you can see the tide pools glisten,
>   see them ripple
>   as the starfish
>   tiptoe in to swim.
> In the tidepools, by the boulders,
> sun pours on their starry shoulders.
> Swaying waters, will I leave you?
> Dancing waters, will you let me,
>   ocean waters?

Poppy would wander in and out of the room handing Tim stuffed animals and dolls and kitchen spoons, while

Koko would sit in the big rocking chair swinging back and forth gently. Barbara's smile would catch him from time to time and the music would flow past him, making him feel not homesick, but at home.

It was during those peaceful evenings that Koko would feel most inspired to talk about his life among the otters. Tim, Barbara and Miles would listen attentively as he told them about Weela and Theo, about the extraordinary life of the sea, and about the frolicking around the kelp beds. One time Koko tried to tell them about Amla, but his words never quite seemed to describe what he was feeling.

"It's all right, Koko," Barbara reassured him. "It's usually the most special things that are hardest to describe."

"It'll come to you," Tim added encouragingly. "You can tell us then."

Koko nodded.

"Amla," Tim mused. "Where have I heard that word before?"

Barbara thought a minute. "There's a shampoo at the health food store called Amla. It's made from Amla berries."

Koko was laughing. "Amla is not shampoo," he said.

Occasionally Barbara would bring out the little cassette tape recorder and would record all of their conversations. "Someday we can play all of this back and enjoy all the things we used to say," she would explain.

Koko knew that when summer came once again, Tim would set aside as many days as his work allowed, and the whole family would return to Monterey to vacation there. And so, looking forward to the future, the months passed by quickly for the boy. Though instead of paying attention to the changes of the moon, as he had done while with the otters, now his mind was captivated by changes more close at hand: the shifting to indoor games during the colder days, the replacing of light cotton with warm fuzzy flannel, the hauling in of the potted pine tree and the hanging of ornaments on it, the wonderful exchanging of gifts, and the wearing of black squeaky boots and bright yellow raincoats.

As the children went about their daily games and projects, Tim and Barbara looked on proudly. Miles, who regarded himself as Koko's protector, frequently explained things to him, while Koko somehow managed to look up to Miles and at the same time look over him protectively. Poppy, whose personality seemed to encompass both sweetness and toughness, was hearty enough to participate in some of their rough-tumble games, yet agreeable enough to go on long searching expeditions, looking for this toy or that toy whenever Miles or Koko requested it. Her breathy laugh was completely captivating to every member of the family, and Miles and Koko—and even Tim and Barbara—would often perform clownishly before her in order to evoke her laughter.

Even when the boys were arguing with each other—or for that matter, even when Poppy was screeching angrily at one or both of them—there was a feeling of rightness about Koko's presence. He was one of the family, and he was happy.

"Dada?"

"Yes, Miles."

"Is the sun bigger than the earth?"

"Yes, it is."

"Is it bigger than all the planets?"

"Uh huh."

"Even bigger than Mars and Mercury?"

"Yup."

"How about Goofy?"

Tim could hardly keep from laughing. Miles seemed so sincere. What could be possibly mean by such an absurd question?"

Barbara's laughter drifted in from the kitchen. "I think he means Pluto," she said.

"Yeah, that's it!" Miles exclaimed. "I always get those two mixed up."

On the north side of their house, bordering the colorful bougainvillea bushes, was an attractive English-style house that belonged to an elderly couple. Their little brown Chihuahua could often be heard disturbing the silence as he barked at imaginary invaders coming from the canyon.

On the south side there was a large, fenced-in lot, which was empty except for an abundance of blackberry bushes that grew so wide there was scarcely any room around them for walking. Several times in the early fall, Miles and Koko had climbed over the tall wooden fence that surrounded the lot and had spent hours collecting the tart, juicy berries. Only once had they brought Poppy along with them. This they accomplished by pulling on the bottom of a loose fence board and then pushing her through the narrow opening that was left between the adjoining boards. But she cried upon discovering that the bushes were thorny, and she ate not only the berries that the boys quickly gathered for her, but also the ones that they gathered for themselves. When that day was over, and Poppy had been safely returned home, they kicked the fence board tightly shut and never invited her again.

Since then, autumn had extended to winter, and then the cold, crisp days of winter had finally given way to spring. The first three weeks of April had been chilly and rainy, giving the children very little time out of doors. Now, at last the rains had stopped, and since Poppy seemed perfectly content to be playing in the wet sandbox by herself, Miles and Koko ran quietly to the south fence and climbed over it.

There had been an absence of ripe blackberries for several months now, and since the boys knew that things grew in the springtime, they were hoping to find that all the little green berry clusters had finally grown and ripened. Jumping down onto the narrow path that encircled the bushes, they searched carefully, first standing on their toes, then bending down low in order to get as many views as possible.

"Well, I guess it's still not time," said Miles disappointedly.

"Here's some that don't taste too bad." Koko handed him a berry that was trying very hard to look black.

Miles' face puckered as he tasted it. "Awfully sour," he said, and just as he spoke he saw what looked to him like a very promising blackberry. It was surrounded by several greener ones and was situated close to the ground, deep inside some matted branches. Climbing over some of the bushes' thorny extensions, he bent over and stretched his arm as far as he could. The berry was too far in. He climbed in even farther and reached again. "I think I got it," he said, and fell into the bushes with a scratchy thump.

"Oh no!" cried Koko, climbing in close to where Miles had fallen. All he could see was the boy's legs as they extended out from the bushes, much as some of the thorny branches did. "Are you OK?"

"Wow, you gotta see this," Miles said as he pulled his legs into the bushes after him. "Wow," he repeated.

And presently, "Wow," whispered Koko, now kneeling by Miles' side, for they had discovered an enormous cave.

This cave had green, leafy walls that had grown out of the

ground, leaving a long wide space between them. First reaching straight up toward the sky, the cave walls had gradually slumped and leaned toward one another, so that they barely met at the top, letting the sun's light trickle in through them.

At the floor of the cave, beginning just in front of where the boys were kneeling, was an enormous puddle—large enough perhaps to be called a pond. The air was almost swampy, and all around them, the boys could hear the skittering and buzzing of bugs and flies.

"Maybe there's cement under the pond, kind of like a swimming pool," said Miles, "and that's why the bushes can't grow in it."

"Maybe," answered Koko distantly, less interested in the mechanics of how the cave had formed itself. "Let's go in the water," he said enthusiastically, pulling off his tennis shoes.

"OK," agreed Miles, taking off his own shoes and slowly crawling into the water as Koko was now doing. "It's a good thing we're wearing shorts," he said, sounding like his own mother.

As they slowly moved into the deeper part of the pond, all around their legs and wrists they could feel hundreds of tiny tadpoles squirming. In the busy bases of the cave walls, they saw frogs hopping here and there among the branches. There were several large brown rocks that emerged from the water near the middle of the pond. As Miles and Koko approached these rocks, four brownish frogs jumped off them and swam toward the sides of the cave nervously.

"Gee, I didn't even see them," Miles exclaimed. Looking beyond the large rocks, "Wow, there's even lily pads," he added.

Just behind the lily pads, at the far end of the cave, there was an enormous, wide rock whose many layered surfaces resembled stairs. On its highest and widest step was a large grayish-green frog. It sat there motionless, except for the movement caused by its own breathing.

"Maybe it's sick," suggested Miles.

"Maybe," Koko replied.

"Hey, this is deep enough to swim!" exclaimed Miles, noticing that where he was kneeling the water came to his upper thighs. "Well, at least we can float," he added as an afterthought. Miles remembered the leather bag full of marbles that was attached to the top of his shorts. "I gotta find a good place for these," he said and started undoing the hook that the bag hung from. These marbles were his treasures. "Boy, I'm glad I remembered about these," he said, and handed the bag over to Koko. "Can you put this over there on that rock next to you?" he asked.

"Sure," said Koko and placed the bag on the rock's gently sloping surface. But the bag slipped, and when Koko reached into the water to pull it out, he grabbed it from the wrong end and all the marbles came rolling out of it.

"Uh oh," sighed Koko, then reached his hands into the water over and over again. "I can't find them," he exclaimed.

If Miles had been at home, he would surely have been crying by now, in this way encouraging Tim or Barbara to come to the rescue. But in this distant setting, all he could do was sit in the water, his eyes cast downward, his lower lip quivering slightly.

"I'm sorry, Miles," said Koko.

"If you look toward the middle of the pond you will find them," said the frog, still sitting on the large rock where they had first seen him.

"Who said that?" asked Miles in a shouting whisper, as he looked back toward the cave entrance.

"You see, the pond is much deeper in the center, and everything tends to roll or slide in that direction."

Now Miles looked at Koko, whose eyes were intent upon the frog.

"I have found several misplaced pebbles that way," the frog stated.

"It's the frog! It's talking!" shouted Miles excitedly.

But Koko was less amazed by the frog than he was by the fact that Miles could hear the frog. During the winter, Tim and Barbara had taken them to a zoo, and while Koko had engaged in a very rewarding exchange of ideas with a resident seal, Miles had remained completely oblivious to the communication.

"Didn't you hear it talk?" asked Miles excitedly.

"Well, actually it isn't so much talking as it is thinking loudly," responded the frog.

"But I can see your mouth moving," said Miles, addressing the frog directly for the first time.

"Oh," the frog chuckled, looking at the boys. "I'm just doing that for your benefit."

"Oh," replied Miles, wondering to himself what the word "benefit" meant.

"Where did you learn English?" asked Koko.

"Oh, here and there," answered the frog. "In people's backyards, at family picnics."

"Do all frogs speak English?" asked Miles.

"We frogs have a language of our own of course," he replied, "but there are those of us with a natural talent for acquiring languages." The frog looked quite pleased with himself.

"You speak it real good," commented Miles. "Almost as good as us."

"Humm," said the frog. "Well, let me introduce myself. My name is Ra... Rah... Rah..." His mouth opened into an enormous yawn. A fly that had been buzzing around nearby flew inadvertently into the frog's mouth an instant before it snapped shut. Miles wondered why a fly would volunteer for such a mission. The frog gulped. "Nir," said the frog.

"Your name is Neer?" asked Koko.

"Ranir," corrected the frog. "I could have sworn I said the 'Ra'."

"I think maybe you did," said Miles, "but we forgot."

Just then, several other frogs came swimming toward the large rock where Ranir was sitting, and they started nervously climbing up onto its many layered surfaces. As they gathered, in a restless brownish group, they mumbled among themselves in a language that neither of the boys could understand. Ranir looked at all of them, then looked at the boys again.

"It is really quite timely that you have come," he said. "You see, we are finding ourselves in somewhat of an unsettling situation."

At that moment another frog, one that had been sitting quietly on one of the lower ledges, started saying something to Ranir. It spoke in a dissatisfied tone, and although neither of the boys could understand what it was saying, they could plainly see that the frog was upset. Several times during its

"…there are those of us with a natural talent
for acquiring languages."

discourse, it pointed nervously to the boys, then turned to look at the other frogs, some of whom seemed to be nodding in agreement.

"As I was saying," continued Ranir, "our situation is quite unsettling. You see, for some unaccountable reason, we have experienced an enormous proliferation of wogs this year. Look at the little dears," he said with a tender smile on his face. "There are literally thousands of them."

Miles and Koko looked at the little tadpoles squirming all around them.

"Yeah," said Koko, "there's almost more of them than there is water."

"Precisely," said Ranir. "And this means that we must have our wog-turning ceremony much earlier this year instead of waiting until late summer, which is when we usually have it."

Miles and Koko listened quietly.

"But the problem is that the berry clusters, which are such an important part of our ceremony, are not yet ripe. And...."

The frogs looked quite uneasy as they huddled close to a little gray frog who seemed to be translating the conversation.

"Well, we were wondering if we could perhaps impose on you to help us, in exchange for..." He glanced at the other frogs briefly. "...for you being invited to watch our ceremony."

One of the frogs lost its footing and landed sideways in the water. Then, regaining its sense of direction, it swam back to the edge of the rock.

"I think that's the same one that was talking before,"

Miles whispered to Koko.

"As I was about to ask," continued Ranir, "is there any way that you could get us some ripe blackberries?"

"Mom has some red ones in the freezer," replied Koko.

"Red blackberries?"

"They're called raspberries," explained Miles.

"And they have little balls clumped together?"

"Oh yeah," answered Koko. "They're real good."

"Humm, sounds promising." Ranir could almost see all the little polliwogs, each one holding a tiny red ball. "And it certainly would be different," he mused. "Would it be possible for you to bring the berries to us? Do you have a lot of them?"

"I saw two whole boxes."

"Sure we can!" said the boys enthusiastically.

"Only they're all frozen," added Miles as an afterthought.

"If you bring them to us tonight," pondered Ranir, "by early morning they should be thawed enough for us to disassemble them."

"Yeah, they melt pretty fast," Miles acknowledged.

"Well, wonderful!" Ranir smiled at them. "I believe we've made a deal. Now, if you will come here tomorrow in the late afternoon, we will have a special place for you to sit and enjoy the ceremony. In fact," Ranir looked thoughtful. "Yes, it should be possible!" he went on. "We will translate one round of our wog-turning song into English, just for you."

"Wow," said the boys almost at the same time.

The frogs had become unsettled again. This time it was a

different frog that was doing the talking. And judging by the way the other frogs kept nodding their heads, it was apparent that the frog was expressing their views faithfully. As it spoke, its grayish brown body kept rising and falling, as if the frog were preparing to hop, while its voice rose higher and higher until it was impossible for the boys to even hear it. Finally, the frog plopped down on the same spot where it had been all along and just sat there panting.

"We just want you to know," stated Ranir, "that this is a most solemn occasion, as the little wogs enter upon froghood only once in their lives. So we would appreciate it very much if you would, um..." He glanced at the other frogs who were looking at him and nodding. "If you would wear clean shirts and shorts for the occasion. And, in order to prevent any sort of mishap, if you would tell no one else about this."

"I know," said Miles. "Things like this can get big people all mixed up."

"You have a good point," said the frog.

"But how about Poppy?" Koko asked suddenly. He was imagining her delighted smile upon seeing so many frogs and polliwogs.

"Yeah, we could squeeze her in through the fence!" added Miles enthusiastically.

With this latest proposal, three more frogs toppled into the water.

"Er," said Ranir, "is Poppy the, er, less mature one with the large legs who often plays in your yard with you?"

"Yeah, she's our little sister," answered Koko.

The frogs were now in a state of total upheaval.

"I'm sure the child is quite charming, really," began Ranir. "It's just that, well I'm sure it was just an unfortunate accident, one of those rare turns of fate, and of course she surely has matured a lot since then...but you see, she, um, sat on one of the members of our family and, well, I'm sure you can understand why we would prefer that she...."

"Yeah, I know," sighed Miles. "That's why Mama calls her the little hippo."

That night the boys tossed and turned under their flannel sheets for hours.

"Are you sure you threw the raspberries right into the cave?"

"Yes, I'm sure. What if we have a late nap and don't wake up on time?"

"We'll tell Mom we're sleepy right after lunch."

"What if Mom asks us to play with Poppy after our nap?"

"What if it's raining?"

The whispering continued.

But the next day things went smoothly. The boys played vigorously with Poppy all morning long, chasing her back and forth across the backyard as she shrieked gleefully. Immediately after lunch they sat down to play with her in her little plastic pool. Then, all dripping wet, they went into the kitchen and told Barbara that they were very sleepy because of a bug that had been buzzing around their faces the night before. They quietly went upstairs, where they put on clean dry shorts and T-shirts. As they climbed into their bunks, they could hear Barbara on the other side of the French doors. She was talking to Poppy soothingly while preparing her for her nap. After a short while, all was silent. They knew that Poppy was surely asleep. Neither of the boys slept. They just waited for what seemed like a good long time. Then, carefully opening the French doors, they tiptoed past their snoring baby sister and quickly went downstairs.

Barbara had her sewing machine set up on the dining room table, and she was busily sewing a pocket onto a dress that she had been making.

"Is this late afternoon?" asked Miles.

"Oh, I think so," answered Barbara, looking at her watch.

"Let's go play out back," suggested Koko, pulling on Miles' hand.

"Have a good time," said Barbara. And they were gone.

In what seemed like no time at all, they climbed the south fence and jumped down onto the path that encircled the blackberry bushes. As they slid through the thorny entrance to the cave, they were impressed by how silent it was inside; not even the flies were buzzing. Ranir sat on his huge rock at the far end of the pond, while in the bushes that surrounded the pond, hundreds of frogs were gathered.

"You may go to where we met the last time," Ranir said to the boys.

They took off their shoes, then crawled through the water to the spot where they had first seen him.

"If you will sit down," said the frog, "I think you will be more comfortable, as it may take a long time."

The boys sat down in the marshy water, their legs loosely

crossed in front of them. The water came up to just below their shoulders. There were large rocks just behind them and to the sides of them, while directly ahead of the boys were the shiny green lily pads. Two of the lily pads were occupied, each by a brownish frog. In front of each of these two frogs, carefully placed on top of their respective lily pads, was a single red raspberry. Five or six feet beyond the lily pads, sitting on his huge layered rock, was Ranir.

Several frogs plopped into the water and swam toward the layered rock. Climbing up onto it, they started gently pushing on a mountain of green leaves, which was just to one side of Ranir and a little behind him. As the leaves fell into the water, what remained was a large red mound made up of thousands of tiny raspberry beads. Except for a few isolated oohs and ahs coming from the sides of the cave, all was silent.

"Sure is quiet," whispered Miles.

"Sssh," hushed Koko.

"We are very grateful to you boys for keeping the silence," stated Ranir in a soft tone. "Now, if you will be very still, the ceremony will soon begin."

Koko had noticed when they first sat down in the marshy water, that he could see and feel hundreds of little polliwogs squirming all around him. Now, as he looked into the water, he saw only a few, and even these were becoming less and less numerous as they swam past him toward the cave entrance. Presently the water was completely still. It was then that the music started.

At first the boys didn't hear it, for its sound was so muted that it seemed to be coming from their own minds, like the faint memory of a song. Then, very gradually, it grew louder and clearer, though always maintaining a soothing quality. It was the sound of voices, much like children's voices, only softer and more slippery. The voices flowed to a steady rhythm. As Koko and Miles glanced to the sides, they saw neat rows of polliwogs—three rows to the left of Koko, and three to the right of Miles—gliding smoothly across the water toward the giant layered rock. The boys couldn't understand the words whose sounds flowed together so smoothly it was hard to tell where one word ended and another started. It was like listening to silk. The polliwogs on Koko's side would sing a phrase; then that phrase would be answered by the polliwogs on Miles' side.

> An da fren sar feem sai tevi
> Las va ranis gamesh revi
> An da fren, sar feem sai,
> An di vey en datensai
> An da fren, sar en feem,
> En va quaris nos aveem

As the polliwogs drew closer to the large rocks, their two sets of rows merged into one wide column from which, six by six, the polliwogs swam toward the rock where Ranir was sitting. Two smaller frogs sat by his side. Whenever a group of six polliwogs approached, each of the three frogs tossed two red raspberry beads into the water. Each polliwog darted toward one of the tiny red balls, and either held it between its lips or, if it was a very mature polliwog, embraced it with its new forelegs and then swam to either side of the cave where hundreds of its relatives could be seen waving proudly.

> An en da, fren en sar,
> Tas va andas amavar
> An en da, daten fren
> Aspris tran en vren en ren

Occasionally a little red bead would get stuck on one of

the lower layers of the large rock, and one of Ranir's two assistants would hop down to dislodge it.

> An en da
> > Ran en ra
> Daten an
> > Ra en ran

Then the voices of all the polliwogs joined together:

> Ga va an
> Va guarai an
> Jamalai an

The singing ended. The column of polliwogs came to a stop as each polliwog swam a tiny bit forward, then a tiny bit backward, in order to maintain its place in the neatly formed column. Koko thought he could hear the song faintly in the background, then realized it was his own remembering of it. Then, as if it had been planned that way, the crickets started chirping—first a few of them, then what must have been hundreds of them. And as the chirping grew louder and louder, Ranir's gray-green frog body started expanding and contracting. With each contraction, a hushing sound reverberated throughout the cave:

> Shmm,
> Shmm,

The sound seemed to be coming from his lungs more than from his mouth. And presently,

> Shmm,
> Shmm,

echoed the sounds of all the surrounding frogs now following Ranir's example. Looking upward, Miles was astonished to see that there were thousands of them, perched like prehistoric birds on all of the cave's branchy walls.

Shmm,

Shmm,

The hushing sound grew louder and louder until the boys thought it could not grow any more. Then, just as suddenly as he had started, Ranir stopped. And when this happened, everyone else stopped. Even the crickets became silent. Everyone seemed to be waiting. Very very softly, the music started again,

An da fren sar feem sai tevi

and with it the procession of polliwogs continued.

Las va ranis gamesh revi

And so the cycle of singing, then silence, then chirpings, then shmms, repeated itself several times; and each time that the cycle was completed, Miles and Koko found themselves hoping it would start again. It was at the end of about the fourth cycle, as the boys waited expectantly for the next repetition, that they noticed that the music had a new quality to it.

"Hey, it's in English!" whispered Miles.

A big smile came over each of the boys' faces as they listened to the English translation.

One, two, three, four, five, six, seven,
All the woggies grow toward Reven,
One, two, three, four, five, six,
One day old or twenty-six,
One, two, three, four and five,
This is why we leap and dive,

The polliwogs sang in the same left to right pattern that they had followed all along.

One and two, three and four,
       On the path to more and more,
One and two, two and three,
       Bounding strong and true and free,
One and two,
       me and you,
One and two,
       you and me,

The voices blended,

       To the One,
       The springing One,
       The endless One.

By now, every single polliwog had received a little red raspberry bead, and while some of these polliwogs swam in the water nibbling on the tasty morsels, others who had already finished eating continued with the singing, so that after several repetitions the boys felt that they knew the song by heart.

The two frogs who had so patiently been sitting on their lily pads, each one tending to a single raspberry, pushed the berries into the water and plunged in after them. Then holding the berries between their taut lips, they swam toward the boys.

"Those are for you," shouted Ranir over the singing.

"Thank you," cried the boys, each one taking a red berry and biting into it. Then, as though the tasting had been the cue, all at once everyone stopped singing, and like an unexpected thunderstorm, thousands of green and gray and brown frogs came falling out of the sky and splashing into the water, making loud croaking noises as they fell.

There was no helping it. Neither of the boys could keep

from laughing, and as they laughed, all of the frogs and polliwogs laughed right along with them. The only problem was that the boys couldn't stop. It was as though their capacity for mirth had been charged and re-charged throughout the entire ceremony, and now that it was finally being expressed, there was no end to it.

"We placed more raspberries for you just at the entrance to our pond," explained Ranir, laughing as he talked. "Enjoy your treat before leaving, my wogs, and come visit us again soon. Now, it's time for our rest."

The boys, still laughing uncontrollably, got up onto their hands and knees, and crawled back toward the entrance of the cave. Sitting at the water's edge and eating the tasty berries, they could still not refrain from laughing. As they looked here and there throughout the cave they could see hundreds of frogs sitting quietly with smiles on their faces. Soon, between bursts of laughter, the boys were yawning. The raspberries were all gone, except for two that had rolled toward Miles' side of the cave. Using his elbow to support his own weight, Miles leaned over to reach them. His elbow slipped and he fell on the ground where he remained fast asleep.

"Miles, Koko, time for dinner!"

"Oh no!" Koko exclaimed, then started shaking Miles by the shoulder.

"What happened?" Miles asked in a startled voice.

"We fell asleep. It's late."

"But look!" shouted Miles, pointing excitedly toward the back of the cave. For just above the huge layered rock sat

Ranir, floating in midair, one leg hanging slightly lower than the other.

"Wow!" exclaimed Koko.

"How's he doing that?" asked Miles.

"Koko, Miles!"

"I don't know. We'd better go."

Koko couldn't sleep. The frogs' ceremony with all of its water and water animals had stirred up memories of his own otter family and friends. He wondered how they were, if they thought of him, and if they were safe.

Looking up to the bunk above him, he could see Miles' hand hanging over the edge and he could hear his heavy breathing. He was fast asleep. The French doors were open, and looking through the wide doorway, he could see Tim curled up on the bed, with Barbara's long slender form under the blankets next to him. Everyone was asleep.

Koko knew that he was only supposed to talk to his immediate family about the otters. But perhaps if he could just spend some time by the pond, in the company of Ranir, he would feel somehow closer to Weela and Theo.

Tiptoeing past the large bed where Tim and Barbara and Poppy were sleeping, he carefully opened the bedroom door, then slowly walked down the hall. Very quietly he went down the stairs, opened the back door and headed toward the south fence. The moon was almost full. Surrounded by its light, he had little difficulty getting over the fence or finding his way into the frogs' cave.

The moon's light trickled softly through the cave's thin

top branches. At the far end of the cave, sitting on his large layered rock, was Ranir.

"What is 'Reven'?" whispered Koko, kneeling at the edge of the pond.

But Ranir didn't answer.

Koko asked his question once again, only this time a little more loudly.

Still there was no answer.

The boy started to turn in order to leave.

"She is well," said Ranir. "They are all well. A new little one grows within her."

Koko turned his glance toward Ranir, wondering if he had heard him correctly.

"You are fortunate indeed to have so many loving parents," said the frog. "Now go. If your mother finds you missing, she will worry."

After breakfast, while Poppy was playing in the living room, the boys once again slipped away and ran to the south fence. Skillfully climbing over it they jumped down onto the narrow path and headed for the cave. Miles toppled into the cave first. Then Koko, who was more graceful, slid through its thorny entrance so smoothly that even the leaves seemed undisturbed.

"Look. My marbles!" exclaimed Miles, for right at the edge of the pond, in a long neat row, were all the marbles that he had lost on his first visit. "Wow, I'd forgotten all about them," he said as he picked them up one by one and tossed them into the leather bag that was lying on the ground next to them.

Koko had already taken off his shoes and was preparing to crawl through the water toward Ranir.

"Come on," he urged.

Soon both boys were once again comfortably situated before Ranir whose motionless eyes didn't seem to notice them.

"I wonder if he's asleep," whispered Koko very softly.

"Thank you for the marbles." Miles' whisper was louder than Koko's.

"Oh, so you've come back," said the frog. "I was wondering when you'd return." He didn't mention Koko's earlier visit.

"What is 'Reven'?" asked Miles.

"So! You are curious about our wog-turning song, are you?" He smiled at the boy. Then, looking at both of them, he said, "We were all quite pleased with the English translation. Perhaps we may even use it for future ceremonies. Did you boys enjoy the ceremony?"

"Oh yes," answered Koko. "It was beautiful."

Ranir seemed very pleased. "You know," he uttered in a low tone, "we are very grateful to you boys for having helped us as you did."

"Oh, that's OK," said Miles.

"What does it mean 'the springing one'?" asked Koko.

"Ah," sighed Ranir. "I had some problems with my translation at that point. 'Springing' seemed to be the closest word I could find, though in our amphibian language the word that we use actually has three meanings, all of which are quite important. It means: always there to hop in and help upon being invited. It also means: always willing to sit back and wait if not invited, thus preparing to hop in, or spring in, at some future time. And lastly, it means having an irresistibly tender quality, which springs up from within and sooner or later evokes an invitation."

Ranir looked at the boys and saw that their faces had expressions of complete bewilderment.

"Well, in any case," he continued, "there was one other word in your English language that I felt...sorely tempted to use, instead of 'springing' that is. Its true meaning comes much closer to that of our frogine word. But unfortunately it is a word which has been so misused by humans that I was afraid it would be misunderstood."

"Yeah," said Miles. "I never heard it before. Besides, it's kinda long."

"Humm?"

"'Springing' is a lot shorter and sounds a lot better than 'sorlytemped.'"

Koko wondered if the word 'Reven' also had several meanings. He was about to ask that very question when Miles inquired about something else that Koko was equally curious about.

"How do you float up in the air?"

"Oh, you saw that, did you?" The frog was smiling. "It's very simple, really. As easy as hopping up, and then just pausing a while before plopping down."

"But how do you keep from falling down?" asked Koko.

"It's just a matter of practice," answered Ranir. "Once you get the feel of it, it's really no harder than keeping from falling up." He paused.

"But why were you so still?" asked Miles. "If you fell asleep way up there, wouldn't you fall?"

Ranir laughed, "I dare say I would fall, and," he whispered under his breath, "occasionally I have fallen." He chuckled to himself. "It is fortunate that I am an aquatic creature who doesn't mind the sudden feel of cold water."

"So why were you so still, then?" repeated Miles, who never let go of a question until he was completely satisfied with the answer. "Were you just getting sleepy?"

Ranir thought for a moment.

"Being very still is just a frog's way of making things simple," he answered. "It's like asking the crickets to be quiet when we frogs are having a chat. In becoming very still, even our eyes settle down and stop gazing this way and that. You see, when it comes to such unmuscular events as floating in the air, the eyes can say the most discouraging things, like 'But you don't have wings!' or..." Ranir looked down at his own greenish belly, "'You've swallowed far too many bugs to be lifting off today!' Well, from the point of view of the eyes, the whole thing is completely impossible, isn't it?"

"I'll say," answered Koko. "After we got home last night, I wondered if it was all a dream."

"So you understand my point, then; it's quite, quite impossible. Unless we become very still and go by what we know inside, instead of by what we see. Did your mother miss the raspberries?"

"She hasn't said anything," answered Miles.

"I hope it doesn't cause any upset."

"Oh, it's OK." Koko's tone was reassuring. "Lots of times

we take things and eat them."

"I'm glad," responded the frog. He yawned.

"Could you teach us?" asked Miles.

"Teach you?"

"How to float in the air."

Now Ranir was laughing heartily. "The problem is, my boys, that the techniques we use are designed especially for frogs, and I'm not at all sure that they would work for humans. Besides," he added in a more serious tone, "it could even be dangerous."

Both boys looked at him intently.

"You might grow webs between your toes. Or your skin might turn brown, or gray , or even green." Ranir looked up at the cave walls thoughtfully. "No," he said. "I simply could not risk it."

"Then how can we ever learn it?" asked Miles unhappily.

Ranir sat quietly. It was obvious that he was deeply involved in thought. "My wogs," he said in a soft voice, "you are very young. Every species has its own way of embracing the powers of nature. Surely in time you will find your own teachers."

Ranir's words had reminded Miles of something.

"Dada says that if you are very close to nature, you can do almost anything."

"Humm. And how are things at home? Are you happy together?"

"Oh, sure," Miles replied, "unless we've done something bad."

"Well you see then," stated the frog, "you've had teachers with you all along, and you didn't even know it." Ranir yawned again.

Miles tried to imagine his parents teaching him how to float in the air. "But I don't think they know how," he said.

"What?" asked Ranir. He sounded a little startled, as though he had just been awakened. Then, looking into Miles' earnest eyes, he said, "Well, perhaps they do or perhaps they don't. But certainly they know other more important things." Ranir's voice was slowing down. "You'd be surprised the things your parents know," he added. "You'd be very sur...."

Koko leaned forward and looked at him very closely. "I think he really is asleep this time," he said.

Barbara was washing the dinner dishes. It was a warm summer evening and she was looking forward to turning off the steamy, hot water.

"Barbara?"

It was Tim's voice; he was calling from downstairs in the study.

"Could you come down here please?"

Barbara left the dishes to soak and headed toward the stairs that led to the study. Briefly glancing into the living room, she saw Miles leafing through one of his books. Koko and Poppy were rocking side by side on the wicker rocking chair.

"Dada's calling me," she explained. "We'll both be up in a little while."

She stepped down the carpeted stairs and turned left at the hallway. As she entered the study she saw Tim, who was standing next to the round oak table and was holding a piece of paper in one hand. When he saw Barbara, he walked toward her and gently put his other hand on her arm, just below her shoulder.

"I think I've found something," he said.

Several weeks earlier, Tim had called the editor of the Santa Cruz newspaper. He had told him that he was writing a book about boating in northern California and had asked the editor if any articles had been written about boating accidents in the Santa Cruz/Monterey area. Tim had explained that he wanted to include copies of newspaper clippings in his published work. Now, almost six weeks later, the editor's findings had arrived. The postman had delivered the envelope earlier that day, and Barbara, not noticing the return address, had placed it on the oak table in the study where she always put Tim's mail.

Resting on the smooth, worn surface of that same oak table were several photocopies of newspaper articles. But it was the sheet of paper that Tim was holding in his hand, that he now brought to her attention.

"Take a look at this," he said.

She reached for the sheet of paper and looked at it curiously. It was a photocopy of newspaper article. The article was a short one: it only took up about three inches of one column and two inches of an adjoining column. The headline read: BOATING ACCIDENT OFF SANTA CRUZ COASTLINE. Barbara's hand started to tremble as she read the small black print:

> Wreckage drifting ashore today brought evidence of a fatal boating explosion. A detailed description of the debris

was rushed to the Honolulu police department. Confirmation arrived this morning that the sailing vessel belonged to Terry Petersen, age 39, and his wife, Tayako, age 37, formerly Tayako Myashiro. Mr. Petersen, a carpenter by trade, and also a boating enthusiast, was going to California in response to a job opportunity. The family set sail from Ala Wai Harbor on May 10. Aboard with Mr. and Mrs. Petersen was their five-month-old son, Yoshi. The explosion is thought to have been caused by an accumulation of gas in the boat's cabin due to a faulty valve in the boat's....

Barbara's hand was trembling so much that she could no longer read.

"Oh, Tim," she said in a shaky voice, then handed the piece of paper to her husband. "Could you please finish it for me?" She pointed to the place where she had stopped reading. "Starting right there," she said.

Tim took the article and started reading aloud.

"The Petersens had no other children. Mr. Petersen's uncle, Mr. Gary Petersen, a retired U.S. Navy officer residing in Florida—the family's only known living relative —has been notified of the tragedy. Memorial services will be held on Sunday, June 8, in Foster Gardens, by Benny and Alicia Johnston, close friends of the Petersens. The service will start at 10 a.m. All friends are welcome."

"Oh, Tim," Barbara said once again, pressing her head against his chest.

"Koko, I've been reading a lot about the sea otters." Tim looked directly at Koko who was sitting across from him at the breakfast table.

"You have?"

"It seems that they are getting a lot more protection than they ever did before."

"Huh?"

"You see," explained Tim, "sea otters eat shellfish, and not too long ago the fishermen got very concerned that there might not be enough left for their businesses."

Koko was almost afraid to ask, "So they shot at the otters?"

"Well, maybe some of them did," answered Tim. "The problem still isn't completely solved but there are a lot of people trying to help the otters," he said in a happier tone, "and several laws are being made to try and protect them from this and other dangers. There's even a group called 'Friends of the Sea Otter' and..."

"I gotta tell Weela," Koko shouted, jumping out of his chair and running to Tim's side. "I don't want to wait until vacation. Oh, please can I go see her today, please?"

It was a three-hour drive to Monterey Bay. Miles was excited, Koko was ecstatic, Poppy was restless as she sat in her car seat, and Barbara was worried. Only Tim looked relaxed as he sat at the steering wheel and listened to his favorite Miles Davis album on the van's stereo system.

To Barbara, Koko was like her new infant baby. It didn't matter that he was four or five years old, or that he could swim like a fish.

She had seen his extraordinary swimming feats at the local swimming pool. It was she who had had to do some quick thinking in order to explain Koko's unique swimming style to other children's parents. Even the lifeguard had been impressed.

"Oh, his aunt told me that he had swimming lessons when he was an infant. I think the lessons were taught by Russians—in Mexico," she had said, and everyone had seemed satisfied with the explanation. But swimming in a heated pool with a lifeguard nearby was one thing; swimming in a cold desolate ocean was another. And since Barbara could not bring herself to refuse the boy, she was going to do the next best thing. She was going to worry.

When they arrived at the beach, Poppy was fast asleep. Barbara unstrapped her safety belt and, carrying her in her arms, followed the others as they ran to the water's edge. It was early in the afternoon. The day was sunny, but also crisp and windy.

Koko stepped out of his beach shoes and pulled off his shirt, leaving on only his red swimming trunks. He looked at Barbara.

"I'll be back before sunset," he assured her, then gave her a big hug. Next he embraced Tim. Finally, smiling at Miles, "See you later," he said in a loud whisper and ran into the water.

When Poppy woke up, she was delighted to discover that she was not in the car anymore. She and Miles played happily in the sand, the hoods of their sweatshirts pulled over their heads to protect their ears from the wind. Tim held Barbara in his arms.

"Don't worry," he said to her. "He'll be fine."

Presently Barbara pulled out the sandwiches and milk that she had quickly packed before leaving the house. She saved one sandwich for Koko.

The hours went by quickly for Miles and Poppy but much more slowly for Barbara and Tim.

"If he doesn't come back, I don't know what I'l do," she confided to Tim as the day wore on.

"He'll come back, I just know it," he answered.

The sun's bright golden rim was almost touching the water's surface. Even Miles was now saying, "Is it time yet, Mama? When's he coming back?"

"Look!" exclaimed Tim. "I think I see him. See, way out there?"

"Where?" asked Miles. "I don't see anyone." And then a little later, "Oh yeah, that's him all right."

"Thank God!" Barbara sighed, now holding tightly onto her husband's arm.

Koko dragged himself out of the water. After taking a few tired steps on the sand, he fell on his knees to rest. He was shivering. Tim threw a beach towel over his shoulders. Koko looked up at them and smiled.

"I have a new baby sister," he said.

That night, as Koko lay in his warm, cozy bunk, a steady stream of memories flowed past him. He recalled Weela and Theo, bursting with happiness upon seeing him. He remembered the joyful squeals of his otter friends as he greeted them near the kelp beds. He relived the sharing of his discovery about the fishermen and the good news about "Friends of the Sea Otter." Koko replayed in his mind all that he had communicated to his otter parents about his wonderful human family. He sighed upon recalling the soft, cuddly feel of his newest baby sister, Sashi. On and on the memories flowed, so that anyone looking in on the resting boy would have seen his face continually curling up in smiles.

As he became more and more drowsy, the memories became less distinct until all that was left was their comforting, flowing feeling. It was then that the old familiar glow came over him once more.

"Amla," he thought.

"Amla," it whispered, and in its radiance he felt the presence of Weela, Theo, Herme, and Sashi.

"Amla," it vibrated like a whispering song.

"But who is singing it?" he wondered.

Then, as if looking into the fabric of the song rather than listening to the song itself, he saw that it was made up of thousands and thousands of moments. Moments that were scattered over space and time, like stars across the sky. "My young kelp plant," Theo was saying. "This is my great big mountain," he heard Miles' voice. "An da fren sar feem sai tevi," "Koko, are your parents hiding?" "Las va ranis gamesh revi." "Oh please, please don't let..." "There's even a group called 'Friends of the Sea Otter.'" "She is well. A new little one grows within her."

"Of course," thought Koko. "Everyone is singing."

His mind drifted away from the details and into the soothing flow of Amla. On and on into the night it enveloped him like a twinkling blanket. Was all of this his own discovery or was it Weela's doing? He didn't know; it didn't matter.

"Dada says that marine biologists spend all their time near the ocean and learn all sorts of things about sea plants and sea animals. Maybe that's what I'll do," stated Koko.

"Well, I think I'll learn to float in the air like you do, Ranir, or maybe even fly like Superman, so that I can go anywhere and help stop bad guys."

"Or, maybe I'll be a vet, so I can fix animals' bodies when they get broken or sick."

All the while, Ranir laughed heartily. "A charming idea!" he exclaimed one time. "A noble cause," he said a little while later. "Lovely!" "Delightful!" he uttered from time to time.

"Do you really think we can do those things, Ranir?" asked Miles.

"Such natural desires, my wogs—do you think nature could refuse them?"

The boys continued with their talking. They didn't even notice that Ranir was getting drowsy. Presently his mouth opened up into a wide yawn that lasted an exceptionally long period of time. After that, the frog remained very still.

"But Ranir," said Miles. "How about if...Ranir?"

"I guess he fell asleep again," whispered Koko.

The boys started crawling toward the front of the cave. Just as they were about to go through its thorny entrance, they heard a low mumbling sound: it was Ranir's voice. Turning their heads to look back at him, they saw that he was as motionless as they had left him, only now there was a faint smile on his face. Then, very slowly he started to speak:

> "When all of this world's sad and happy events
> seem like shifting clouds,
> and the glow of this vast universe
> shines like a candle in your heart."

Miles' lips were half open. He looked over at Koko. "Reven," he whispered.

*T*im was sitting on the living room sofa, studying some construction plans.

"Does the universe glow, Dada?"

"Yes, Miles, it's a very luminous universe. It glows through and through."

"You mean like in its vitamins and minerals?"

"I guess that pretty much describes it."

"But does it glow inside of us?"

Even Barbara, who was sitting in the dining room cutting out a pattern on some cloth, stopped the movement of her scissors in order to listen.

"We're part of this universe. So it glows inside of us too."

"But I don't see it glow."

Tim put his hand on his son's shoulder. "I think it's something we feel inside, rather than something we see with our eyes," he explained.

"Oh, 'cause the skin is too thick, right?"

"Well, something like that." Tim smiled at him then went back to his studying.

"Dada?"

"Yes, Miles?"

"I don't feel it glow either."

"Well sure you do Miles, like when you're happy or when you're feeling real close to someone."

"Oh, yeah...."

"And, you know what else?"

"What?"

"Since the glow is everywhere, if we could somehow, just kind of sink into it, then we'd be everywhere too."

"Hey yeah, like not stuck anymore."

"That's right."

Miles thought about the way he sometimes felt around Ranir.

"I've felt that way before," he said.

"Yeah, Miles?"

"Uh huh, only not enough."

Tim and Barbara felt as two astronauts would upon discovering that their child shared their same longing for the stars.

"Well, we're working on it, Miles."

"Rumble, rumble, rumble." Miles was dreaming that a giant skyscraper was being built, right in front of their house.

"Rumble, rumble." The bulldozers hummed as they leveled the ground.

He opened his eyes and the sound of bulldozers continued. He climbed down the bunk bed's ladder and ran to the bedroom window.

"Oh no! Look what's happening!" he shouted, waking up Koko, who had been asleep.

"Oh no!" shouted Koko; for there really were bulldozers at work, and they were busily clearing away all of the bushes in the vacant lot.

Tim and Barbara came running in to see why the boys were shouting.

"They're tearing everything down!" Koko said tearfully.

"It's all right," Barbara consoled him. "We'll get some blackberry bushes and plant them in our own back yard."

"I guess they're going to be building a house," commented Tim. He wondered to himself which company would be building it.

"But Ranir," Miles sobbed.

"Who's Ranir?" asked Tim.

"A frog we know," Koko replied. "He lives in the bushes."

"Frogs are very smart," Tim reassured. "He'll be all right. I bet he's long gone by now."

Later that day, when Miles and Koko looked over the fence, they found that all the blackberry bushes were gone. Even the pond had been completely leveled and filled in with fresh new dirt.

Neither of the boys had been feeling very cheerful. In fact, at one point they had seemed so despondent that Barbara had put Poppy in the stroller and had walked with them to the nearest shopping center, where she bought them an enormous box of tinker toys to add to their existing collection.

That evening, after dinner, she and Tim had spent almost two hours with the boys, sitting in the living room and building giant tinker robots that were almost as tall as the boys were. Even Poppy had contributed to the project, by constructing several odd-shaped robot arms and robot antennae. Miles and Koko had actually managed to laugh a few times, but Tim and Barbara could plainly see that the boys' feelings about their frog friend ran very deep.

Late that night, as the boys lay in their beds fast asleep, they were awakened by a thumping sound near the bedroom window. Koko climbed out of his bunk and ran to the window to see.

"It's Ranir!" he exclaimed in a loud whisper, then pushed upward on the window frame, making the window open.

"Ranir!" shouted Miles, climbing down the bunk bed'ladder.

The frog was sitting on the windowsill, panting.

"Are you all right?" asked Miles, kneeling on the floor in order to see the frog more closely.

"I'm fine," Ranir answered. "Fine. Though it has been quite a day, quite a day indeed."

"How did you get up here?" asked Miles.

"I just climbed the tree." The frog pointed at the large oak whose branches extended to just below the bedroom window.

"Where are all the frogs?" Koko asked, now sitting on the floor, right next to where Miles was kneeling.

"Oh, here and there," the frog replied. "Though most of us have gathered in a lovely spot about five houses away from here." Ranir pointed northward. "It's a large, spacious back yard; and it has blackberry bushes. I think we will be very happy there."

"What about the tadpoles?" asked Miles.

"The poor wogs," sighed Ranir, "caught in such pandemonium while still being too young to travel on their own. But," he added in a higher pitch, "we managed to move them to several nice puddles, here and there. Once they get their hopping legs, they can join us."

"How did you move them?" asked Miles, who was always concerned with the mechanics of how things happened.

"Each of us frogs carried one wog," he said, "in the space between our shoulder blades."

"Wow...." Miles tried to picture it in his mind.

"Which brings me to the reason for my visit." The frog paused awhile, as if to give emphasis to his next words. "We left several hundred wogs in your little sister's plastic pool, in your backyard. And I wanted to ask you boys if you would please pull the pool into the shade tomorrow, as too much sun is not good for their health."

"Oh sure, we can do that," replied Koko.

"Also, I wanted to ask you...well, I realize that she has matured a great deal since then, but just to be on the safe side, could you..."

"It's OK," Miles interrupted, "we'll make sure Poppy doesn't squish them."

Ranir let out a sigh of relief. "Thank you! Now I can go to our new home in complete confidence."

"When will we see you again?" asked Koko.

"Well, I don't know," answered the frog. "You see, our new home is quite far from here, and there's so much organizing to be done now that we've moved. And then of course there's the problem of the large beast that lives next door to you."

"What large beast?" asked Miles.

"I think he means the O'Gradys' Chihuahua," explained Koko.

"Oh."

"He bit a hole right into one of my webs this evening," Ranir continued, raising his right hind foot and looking at it.

"Are you going to be all right?" Koko started to lean forward in order to get a closer look at the injury.

"Oh, most assuredly!" the frog replied. "Fortunately, it was only a small puncture wound. But the beast is certainly no one to tangle with."

"Each of us frogs, carried one wog," he said,
"in the space between our shoulder blades."

"So when are you coming back?" Miles inquired.

Ranir took a deep breath. "I will try to come back, my boy, but I can't promise."

"But I want you to come back!" Miles' lower lip was quivering slightly.

"Come, come, my boy," Ranir began in a soothing tone, but before he could say any more, Miles put his head down on the windowsill and started to cry.

"It's OK, Miles...." Koko placed his hands gently around Miles' shoulders.

Ranir took several deep breaths and waited for the boy's crying to subside. Then, when it had finally turned into a soft whimper, he said, "Let me tell you something very special."

Miles slowly raised his head and looked at Ranir. "What is it?" he asked.

Ranir spoke softly. "Every time you meet a frog—any frog," he said, "and you treat that frog with great kindness, so that you finally see what resembles a smile on its face, then you will know, my wog, that right at that moment, I also am smiling at you."

"Is that really true?" asked Miles, suppressing an urge to cry again.

Ranir looked at him. "Someday you will know just how true it is." He looked through the windows of the closed French doors to where Tim, Barbara, and Poppy were sleeping.

"Yes, my wogs, you are very fortunate—very fortunate indeed!" Then looking at the moon as it peered from behind the clouds, he said, "I have a long way to travel and I'm hoping to reach home before daybreak." He jumped off the windowsill and onto the oak tree. "Don't forget about the wogs!" he shouted, hopping down to one of the tree's lower branches.

"We won't!" Miles called out while standing at the window and watching the frog disappear into the darkness.

Just as Ranir had requested, the boys went out to Poppy's swimming pool the next morning after breakfast; and, holding onto the pool's plastic rim, they pulled it into the shade of the maple tree. Poppy came with them and was delighted to see the polliwogs swimming around in the water, but she never once tried to grab them nor did she hurt them in any way.

Two times after that, Miles and Koko allowed her to sit in the pool and feel the little tadpoles wriggling all around her. She followed the advice of her two older brothers, and didn't splash into the water abruptly. Indeed, she was maturing.

The tadpoles also were maturing and, because they were all at different stages of development, each time that Miles and Koko visited the pool, they would notice that more of them had left. One day, when the boys went to the pool to see them, they found that all of them were gone.

*Two times after that, Miles and Koko allowed
her to sit in the pool and feel the little tadpoles
wriggling all around her.*

The little plastic pool had been sitting unused in the backyard for several days. Since it was almost two thirds full with rainwater, leaves and twigs, Barbara asked Miles and Koko to empty it out. The boys sat on the ground next to the little pool and looked into its murky surface. Koko pulled out a twig and started tapping on the pool's stiff plastic rim.

It was a warm summer morning, late in July. Soon they would be going to Monterey for their beach vacation. This year they would stay there for two months, and Koko would find plenty of time to visit with his family of otters. Then they would be going to Yosemite and camping with the grandmas and the grandpas. Miles was especially excited about this part of the vacation, as he loved all of his grandparents dearly. Finally, when summer was over would come the boys' first year of school.

Koko was tapping out a beat on the pool's rim:

Tap tap tap, pause. Tap tap tap.

It was the same beat that Barbara would tap on the tambourine whenever she did the wog-turning song with them. She had heard the boys voicing it out to one another and had taken a liking to it. She had assumed that the boys had picked it up from one of their frog-puppet TV shows and, being very poetic herself, she had changed some of the words to suit her own sense of flow and meaning.

Tap tap tap, pause. Tap tap tap.

Several weeks earlier, Tim and Barbara had shown the copy of the Santa Cruz newspaper article to Koko. And now the boy knew about his father's uncle who lived in Florida. On this particular summer morning, just before Barbara had asked the boys to empty out the little pool, Tim had suggested to Koko that he might someday want to meet his uncle, perhaps a few months in the future, over the Christmas holidays. Tim and Barbara had decided to present the idea to him in a casual fashion, without bringing up any of the possible drawbacks to such an endeavor. They had wanted to know the boy's basic feelings, completely apart from any concerns or misgivings. Koko's response had been surprising.

"Uncle Gary must be very nice," he had said between bites of pancake, "but I don't think he'll mind if I don't meet him."

This was, of course, the type of answer that Tim and Barbara had been secretly hoping for. Even so, they had felt compelled to probe a little further, just to make sure.

"You know, Koko," Barbara had said hesitantly, "your uncle Gary might be able to tell you a lot about what your first parents were like. He might even have pictures."

Koko had placed his fork gently down on his plate. "I already know what my parents are like, in Amla. Why do I need pictures?"

His words had suddenly reminded them that Koko was no ordinary child, and Tim had groped for words that would at least show the boy their willingness to understand him.

"Well, I guess you really don't need pictures, do you?" he had said awkwardly, then had thought to himself how much there was yet to learn from the boy.

Koko's response had left Barbara feeling much too relieved to even think about saying anything. She had expressed her relief by eating three enormous mouthfuls of pancake, one right after the other.

Miles had also felt relieved, as he hadn't liked the idea of being away from home at Christmastime.

Tap tap tap, pause. Tap tap tap.

Miles was looking at Koko and remembering the morning's conversation.

"I'm glad we aren't going to Florida for Christmas," he said.

"Yeah?"

"I just want us to be here."

"Me too." Koko's expression became thoughtful. "Besides, Uncle Gary might have liked me too much."

"Hey yeah," commented Miles, "and wanted you to stay with him."

Tap tap tap, pause. Tap tap tap.

"Are you scared of school?" Miles spoke again.

"No. Are you?"

"Kind of."

"Why?"

"I guess 'cause Robert, you know, the boy at the playground...he goes to school and he's sort of mean."

"Oh, so what?" Koko shrugged his shoulders. "I won't be mean to you."

Miles couldn't keep from smiling.

"Do you think we'll learn more about Reven at school?" asked Koko.

"I think we'll learn about it at home." His eyes connected with Koko's momentarily. "It just feels that way around Mama and Dada sometimes—kind of like it felt around Ranir."

"Yeah, like when we're all together, talking quiet sometimes."

Miles nodded. "But if Ranir comes back," he added thoughtfully, "then I want to learn about it from him."

After all, how could learning something from one's own parents compare with learning it from a gray-green frog?

A dragonfly hovered over the little swimming pool and then took off, zooming right past Koko's face.

Neither of the boys could sing very well, but they could both keep a beat. Sometimes they would sing the wog-turning song back and forth to one another, much like children do when they shout back and forth asking riddles to which they already know the answers.

"I guess we'd better empty out the pool," said Miles.

"Yeah, I guess so."

Both boys stood up. Then, bending over, they held on tightly to one side of the pool's rim.

"One, two, three, four, five, six, seven!" Koko shouted out the challenge.

"All the children grow toward Reven!" Miles answered it.

The pool was too heavy with water, and they couldn't lift the side of it to tip it.

"One, two, three, four, five, six," Koko chimed again, his voice almost melodious.

"One-year-old or ninety-six," Miles stated decisively.

"One, two, three, four and five,"

"This is why we are alive."

"One and two, three and four," Koko's voice strained a little as the boys once again tried to lift the pool.

"On the path to more and more." Miles was slightly out of breath.

The pool was sitting on a small slope, and now the boys were walking around the pool toward the top of that slope.

"One and two, two and three,"

"Growing strong and true and free."

The boys were now standing on the high side of the pool.

"One and two," they bent over again.

"Me and you." Miles gripped the pool's rim.

"One and two," the boys lifted.

"You and me—now push!" shouted Miles.

The water poured onto the ground making the earth look rich and warm and brown.

"To the One, the springing One, the endless One," they chimed.

There was laughter in their voices as they stamped their feet in the puddles that spread out before them.

To the One,
The loving One,
The endless One.